BETWEEN THE WORLDS

FLAMBARD MODERN CLASSICS

BETWEEN THE WORLDS

Andrée Chedid

Translated by Suzanne Hinton

Liberté • Égalité • Fraternité
RÉPUBLIQUE FRANÇAISE

First published in Great Britain in 2007 by Flambard Press
Stable Cottage, East Fourstones, Hexham NE47 5DX
www.flambardpress.co.uk

Typeset by BookType
Cover Design by Gainford Design Associates
Printed in Great Britain by Cromwell Press, Trowbridge, Wiltshire

A CIP catalogue record for this book is available from the British Library.
ISBN-13: 978-1-873226-88-9
ISBN-10: 1-8732267-88-8

This book is supported by the French Ministry of Foreign Affairs, as part of the
Burgess Programme run by the Cultural Department of the French Embassy in London.
www.frenchbooknews.com

'Introduction' © Suzanne Hinton 2007; 'My Sudanese Lady' ('La Soudanaise') first published in *Les Corps et le Temps* © Flammarion 1978; 'Death in Slow Motion' ('Mort au ralenti') first published in *Mondes, Miroirs, Magies* © Flammarion 1988; 'Dinner with the In-Laws' ('Un dîner en famille') first published in *L'Étroite Peau* © Flammarion 1978/Julliard 1965; 'Born of the Shadows' ('Née des ténèbres') first published in *À la mort, à la vie* © Flammarion 1992; 'Between the Worlds' ('Entremondes') first published in *Mondes, Miroirs, Magies* © Flammarion 1988; 'Those Violets' ('Face aux violettes') first published in *Mondes, Miroirs, Magies* © Flammarion 1988; 'Enduring Patience' ('La longue patience') first published in *L'Étroite Peau* © Flammarion 1978/Julliard 1965; 'Here and Now' ('Face au présent') first published in *A la vie, à la mort* © Flammarion 1992; 'The Boy Beneath the Streetlamp' ('L'Enfant au réverbère') first published in *Mondes, Miroirs, Magies* © Flammarion 1988; 'Time and the Body' ('Les Corps et le temps') first published in *Les Corps et le Temps* © Flammarion 1978; 'Eggs and Improvisation' ('Solfège aux œufs') first published in *Mondes, Miroirs, Magies* © Flammarion 1988; 'One Day . . . the Enemy' ('Un jour . . . l'ennemi') first published in *Les Corps et le Temps* © Flammarion 1978; 'The Door Across the Street' ('La porte d'en face') first published in *Les Corps et le Temps* © Flammarion 1978; 'The Ancestor and His Donkey ('L'Ancêtre sur son âne') first published in *A la mort, à la vie* © Flammarion 1992; 'The Weight of Things' ('Le Poids des choses') first published in *A la vie, à la mort* © Flammarion 1992; 'Brothers in the Long Ordeal' ('Les frères du long malheur') first published in *A la mort, à la mort* © Flammarion 1992; 'Prison' ('La maison de force') first published in *L'Étroite Peau* © Flammarion 1978/Julliard 1965; 'The Motor Horn' ('Klaxon') first published in *Mondes, Miroirs, Magies* © Flammarion 1988; 'The Death of the Porter' ('La mort du portefaix') first published in *L'Étroite Peau* © Flammarion 1978/Julliard 1965; 'The Woman in Red' ('La femme en rouge') first published in *A la mort, à la vie* © Flammarion 1992; 'The Dual-Carriageway' ('Le Grand Boulevard') first published in *L'Étroite Peau* © Flammarion 1978/Julliard 1965; 'The Swing' ('La balançoire') first published in *A la vie, à la mort* © Flammarion 1992; 'The No. 9 Tram' ('Le tramway No. 9') first published in *A la mort, à la vie* © Flammarion 1992; 'The Punishment' ('La punition') first published in *Mondes, Miroirs, Magies* © Flammarion 1988; 'The Woman in the Taxi' ('La femme au taxi') first published in *Les Corps et le Temps* © Flammarion 1978.

Flambard Press wishes to thank Arts Council England for its financial support.

Flambard Press is a member of Inpress, and of Independent Northern Publishers.

Contents

The Author

Andrée Chedid was born in Cairo on 20 March 1920 to Alice Godel and Selim Saab. Her mother's family was from Damascus in Syria, while her father's originated from Baabda in Lebanon. Chedid's upbringing saw her move between Egypt and France, suggesting the origin of her willingness to embrace contrasting cultures and environments in her writing. Her primary education was spent at the Sacred Heart School in Cairo before she moved, in 1934, to a Catholic secondary school in Paris, where she was to remain until returning to Egypt to attend the American University of Cairo. In 1942 she graduated with a BA in Journalism.

When Andrée Chedid's first book was published the following year, she was twenty-three years old and living in Lebanon where her husband Louis was attending medical school. *On the Trails of My Fancy*, a poetry collection, was written in English – an unusual choice of language given the young writer's life so far.

The couple moved to Paris in 1946, where they acquired French citizenship and Louis began work at the Institut Pasteur. At this time, Chedid began to write in her first language, French, and expanded her output to fiction and drama. Her first novel, *From Sleep Unbound*

(*Le sommeil délivré*), was published in 1952, and twenty more have followed. Much of her work has been translated into English and other languages, notably *The Multiple Child* (*L'enfant multiple*, set in war-torn Lebanon), *The Sixth Day* (*Le sixième jour*) and *The Return to Beirut* (*La maison sans racines*). Several collections of short stories and poems have found critical acclaim across the French-speaking world and beyond. She has also written a number of books for children and all four of her plays have been produced for stage or radio.

Chedid has been awarded numerous literary prizes, including Le Prix de l'Académie Mallarmé (1976), Le Grand Prix Paul Morand (2001) and the prestigious Goncourt Short Story Prize (1979). Because her recurring themes remain both universal and constantly topical, her work continues to attract attention and readers, and her books are studied in French and British universities.

The Sixth Day was made into a film by the renowned Egyptian director Youssef Chahine, while many young French pop-music fans will be familiar with the lyrics of the number-one hit single by the singer 'M' – written by his grandmother, Andrée Chedid.

Introduction

A little girl swings high on her garden swing. As she rises level with the top of the garden wall, she glimpses Cairo spread below her. It is a world she cannot reach but which fascinates her ('The Swing'). The short stories of Andrée Chedid reveal to us worlds we do not know or have forgotten: childhood, old age, war, religion, love, hate and all those 'living things which bubble up inside every one of us' (quoted in an interview with Francine Bordealeau).

Andrée Chedid intends to 'keep my eyes open to the suffering, to the misery and to the cruelty of the world'. For the horrors of the Lebanese Civil War, as seen in 'Death in Slow Motion' or 'One Day . . . the Enemy', are the horrors of the suffering of any victim of urban warfare. Men grow old and frail ('Time and the Body'); communities are displaced ('The Dual-Carriageway'); and there are, of course, the tensions between tradition and modernity ('The Ancestor and His Donkey', 'The Boy Beneath the Streetlamp'), between East and West ('The Motor Horn') and between brother and brother ('Brothers in the Long Ordeal').

But if Andrée Chedid writes about subjects which are 'marked by tragedy', the very next words on the author's lips are 'and hope', for if tragedy is the weft of her work, the colourful, hopeful warp is formed by 'the light, the beauty, everything that helps us reach beyond ourselves'. Mme Chedid goes to the essentials of the human condition. A large part of that human condition is to reach beyond our paltry selves. Many of the short stories in this collection show that we can escape ourselves through, amongst many other qualities, compassion ('The No. 9 Tram'; 'Death in Slow Motion') friendship ('My Sudanese Lady') and love ('The Woman in Red'). But perhaps more important than through grandiose sentiments, it is through the small details that the author shows that humankind has every reason to hope rather than despair: the comforting lie to a dying woman ('Death in Slow Motion'); genuine gratitude for the teaching of a sadistic governess ('The Punishment'); admiration for the struggles of an immigrant mother ('Between the Worlds') . . . and yes, you can come to love what you hated at first, even if it is a humble violet ('Those Violets').

In France, Andrée Chedid is considered foremost as a poet and writer on the human condition. There are examples in this collection of poetic reveries which carry the reader along and into the very being of another person ('The Door Across the Street'; 'Born of the Shadows'). In the Anglo-Saxon world this aspect of her work will also be much admired. However, there are two aspects of this collection which will perhaps appeal just as much to the English-speaking reader. Andrée Chedid is a writer of comedy, from the gently humorous ('The Death of the Porter') to the farcical ('Eggs and Improvisation') via the absurd – the bad hair-cut day to end all bad hair-cut days ('Dinner with the In-Laws').

The second aspect that draws the reader in to these stories is their wonderful sense of place. We see few of the great tourist attractions of the world. We see something far more fascinating: the buzz of activity in a Cairo street ('My Sudanese Lady'); a Parisian café terrace brought alive as we read ('Here and Now'); the back streets of Giza, 'behind' the pyramids, as it were ('The Boy Beneath the Streetlamp'); and anything from a magnificent Cairo villa ('Eggs and Improvisation') to a humble hut beside the Nile ('Prison').

Each time the swing rises high above the wall of our own world, each time we read a new story, Andrée Chedid unfolds for us not only her immense understanding of humanity in a beautifully crafted and structured piece of writing, but worlds upon worlds upon worlds.

Suzanne Hinton

My Sudanese Lady

'I have abolished the difference
Between images of myself and the images of others.'
Mayakovsky

U_p there, on the terrace, my Sudanese lady was dying . . .

When I found out, much later, something was wrenched from me, a light guttered. And then this burning remorse came over me for having forgotten her, for weeks and months at a time; for not having been there for her.

I imagined her last imperceptible breath, stifled all the more because she wanted so much not to be a burden on those around her; this thin breath being drawn one last time in her large frame and rising from this flesh and bone fashioned out of its dark, noble clay; I could imagine this breath fluttering then above her terrace before skimming across the teeming city which filled her with dread, and finally, further off, melting away to nothing at the edge of the desert.

*

From her husband, a caretaker in a small, ten-storey block of flats – a striking man yet gentle despite boasting many a scar – I had finally got permission for her to come down from her roof terrace one afternoon so we could go for a walk, like two sisters, in the streets of Cairo.

Since they had arrived from the Sudan – more than twenty years previously – all she had known of the city were those eyries from which she could gaze down, from a distance, at the ever-growing masses of people.

Partially veiled and curled up in the depths of a taxi, she had crossed the town just three times. The first when she had arrived and then twice to change terrace. By moving from a working-class suburb into the heart of the city the caretaker had, little by little, improved his social standing. He even had a bit of a financial interest in the tiny café – overflowing with chairs and tables that spilled out into the alley – tucked away at the foot of the block where he worked.

Getting them to agree to this excursion had not been easy. He – like his wife – believed in the conventions and the prejudices which hold that women are timorous and childlike. My suggestion took them both by surprise.

With a mixture of embarrassment and friendliness she refused at first. I insisted.

'She's afraid,' he said.

'We'll go together. We'll hold hands.'

I described where we would be walking, the passers-by, the shop windows . . . At last I saw a glint in her eyes.

I was nearly thirty at the time; she was eight or nine years older. From the outset, I had an ulterior motive. My life, with its many and varied layers, threw up questions and choices for me; hers was inextricably woven into a rigid pattern. But I felt she was so alive that I was haunted by the desire to pluck her from a slow slide into melancholy.

Her five children were quite different. Especially her daughters, who knew the outside world but did not talk to her about it. For her part, she asked no questions. The two youngest girls were still at school; the third did needlework for an embroideress who took in outwork, several blocks from where she lived.

It seemed a foregone conclusion that my Sudanese lady's life, devoid of any stimulation, would be lived out to the end in this cramped space, hovering between the sky and the tarmac. And that she would spin out her days, sheltered from life's storms, as if borne along on a raft which she would not dream of criticising or of pointing in any other direction.

Her family thought of her with affection and detachment. She often made me think of those rocks which have been worn smooth by water and time and which settle – unchanging and still – at the edge of beaches, whilst the action of the sea continues to wash pebbles and shells over them, making them quiver and change shape and thus resemble all living things.

Bursting into loud laughter – which shook him from head to toe and dislodged his turban, which he straightened before giving me his answer – the caretaker granted my request: 'I've warned you!' he said. 'If things go wrong, I've warned you!'

Over the years, our meetings were few and far between; but our affection was none the less for all that.

Everything about us was different, yet everything bound us together, or rather, what brought us together came from the pleasure – intangible yet delightful – we felt in each other's company.

My Sudanese lady's domain consisted of three rooms which erupted like warts on various corners of the roof terrace. These rooms clung on over a chaos consisting of hens and crates, herbs growing in cooking pots, the goat, ripped suitcases, empty bottles and cans, damaged furniture, a tailor's dummy with an impressive bosom and a radio of which only the outer casing survived.

This junk – constantly being dodged by one or other of them and forever being walked on by the to-ings and fro-ings of the hens, the chicks and the goat – had not been accumulated out of any desire to hoard; not at all. It was scattered round, laid out to make up for when things were in short supply at home, or in one of the homes of people on the other terraces. These people knew that, at any time of day, they could ferret around this scrap heap and take away whatever they needed. My Sudanese lady used only objects which were absolutely essential and coveted no others.

We exchanged barely a few words, she and I. My Sudanese lady spoke mainly her native language; I lived, most of my time, abroad. But these few words were enough for us.

Each time I got back from a trip, without waiting for the lift, which was usually out of order, I would climb the one hundred and twenty-three steps and emerge, unannounced, onto the sunlit roof terrace. The intensity of the light made me blink.

Whatever the time, there she would be! Dressed in black, her hair covered by its square of cloth. She would welcome me with open arms and we would embrace.

In her arms, I would sink into the rich soil of my roots, into the loam of this land which has never stopped being part of me. I have been known, on my return, to go and fetch handfuls of it from the edges of the Nile so I can press my lips to it and linger over it.

Then she would apologise and go off for a few minutes to one of her rooms, leaving me, once more, to gaze at this, my one and only city.

Each time I would see that the façades were more cracked and the streets more crowded; buildings were ever more tumbledown and there was terrace upon terrace on which the quantities of junk grew constantly. Near the horizon I could make out that unchanged desert hill; and then there were those arrows of prayer thrusting up out of each district. Once again I would hear the car horns which in other towns, where such raucousness is prohibited, take me by surprise and

17

suddenly waft me back here, to this vitality and these smells which are so familiar to me.

My Sudanese lady would come out again with her other veil over her hair; this was the length of spotless linen which she kept in honour of her guest. The gleaming white fabric now framed her beautiful, black, beaming face.

Next, she would sit down, her back straight, on the edge of her bed; I would sit opposite her on a chair with a mended straw seat. We would hold hands. It was a ritual, free from formality, that had lost none of its charm over the years.

Her warm, plump hands with their satiny skin squeezed mine on which the veins stood out prominently or else squeezed her own hands together between mine.

Then the words came. Not to break the silence but rather to take its weight.

'Are you all right?' she would say.

'Are you all right?'

The question became the reply and the reply, the question. Then it all began again, slowly, in time with our breathing. We never tired of offering up the same words to each other like crusts of bread when times are hard.

'Are you all right?'

'Are you all right?'

*

I sweep my Sudanese lady along with me through the vast metropolis.

She is wearing brown sandals and the long black robe which flaps around her ankles. Her hair is pulled back from her face round which she has draped the veil she wears on high days and holidays.

Just two women, walking down streets and along avenues, into alleys and over crossroads. We weave our way through the cars. Her arm stiffens and pulls back. Perspiration is running down her cheeks, the sweat on our palms blends together.

We walk along the pavements. Shattered paving stones lay bare the entrails of the earth beneath: pipes padded with rust, a maze of telephone wires which two men, sitting on the edge of the hole, are feverishly attempting to untangle. We step over an oozing drain. We dive into the crowd and then haul ourselves out of it. I sense she is torn between happiness and panic.

A child is yelling out the news headlines; he is running cheerfully after the passers-by and knocking on car windows. Yellow kiosks stand out along the streets, packed with their cargo of cigarettes, sugary drinks and chewing-gum. Safe in his lair a street trader, hunched on his stool, placidly watches the swirls of activity outside. I buy two lemonades, which we drink straight from the bottle.

Broken balconies, cracked walls, grimy windows; bustling, noisy, covered in weals, our city is throbbing with life.

Pushed on by the crowd we go up the steps of footbridges which, suspended a few metres above the ground, criss-cross the vast spaces where vehicles of every sort snarl themselves up. We come down. My Sudanese lady's arm is more and more relaxed, her step more and more sprightly.

She has just let go of my hand. Breathing in the town through all her pores, she is now moving along on her own, her head held high, her back straight.

We buy two apples. I bite into one; she slips hers into the depths of her pocket. We hug the shop windows, some dusty, some spick and span. Shoes are laid out in their hundreds, the flowers look exhausted; the fabrics, artistically draped, make a show of being formal. There is a queue outside the food shop.

The huge body of my Sudanese lady lets itself be carried along by the city's momentum. Her eyes are sparkling. She says to me: 'Are you all right?'

The uproar in the roadway scares and fascinates her at one and the same time. She signals to me that she wants to cross over.

We enter the fray.

Engines judder. Cyclists wobble. A donkey pulling a cart stands stock-still and waits. My Sudanese lady stops to stroke the animal's long ears and its obstinate, gentle face.

Ringed round by the seething swirl of the traffic, deafened by its throbbing movement we step out in a sort of happy stupor.

But suddenly, out of the blue: the senseless accident.

Even today I still wonder how it could have happened.

She was getting further and further ahead of me. There was that glee, that eagerness you see in a swimmer walking into the sea and giving her whole body up to the wind, the sun and the waves . . . then I heard her scream.

The full-throated scream stops me in my track and cuts through the hubbub. All of a sudden and for the first time I see her hair, every strand of it. Then – floating in mid-air, floating away from us at the same speed as the traffic which was now suddenly moving again – I spot her veil. Her light-coloured veil dangling from the back of an enormous red bus.

I can still see that streamer of linen. Carried along by the tightly packed lump of scarlet metal brimming with passengers, its image glows white, ripples in the air, then vanishes whilst my Sudanese lady, rooted to the spot with mortification, spreads her broad hands wide and hides her hair from sight.

It's over in a few seconds. The bus stops as suddenly as it started.

I dash over. I unhook the veil and rush back to her with it.

Hurriedly, she covers up her hair. Head down, she slips her hand in mine.

Saying nothing, she pulls me firmly along, towards the way back home.

*

I never knew quite how, that evening, she told the story of her outing to her family. Nor what role the incident with the veil played in her account. Had she perhaps said nothing about it?

A year later she contracted a contagious disease which weakened her heart.

It was her heart which killed her after her last, short illness.

They told me that, feeling the end was near, she asked for her best veil to be put on her head and that in her last minutes, jumbled up with words from her native language, she said over and over again, with a smile: 'Are you all right?'

For me, the words and the fact that she wanted the veil were a sort of sign. I think it was through them she made me understand that, despite her mishap, she would have set off on more outings, more adventures . . . had she lived.

Up there, on the terrace, my Sudanese lady died . . . and I was far away . . .

Death in Slow Motion

The young woman felt the exact spot where the bullet hit her in the back. The sharp pain stung for a split second.

She carried on walking as if nothing had happened. But the illusion did not last.

All around, the uprooted trees, the pitted roadway, the gaping, burned-out blocks of flats were clear proof that the fighting had been fierce; and, once again, the truce fragile.

M. had just been hit by a sudden burst of fire of which she had not been the target. Her injuries, however, were real enough.

She did not want to know what was happening. The pain had gone. All that mattered now, even more than life, was to get to where he was waiting for her. A fifteen-minute walk from here, at the end of the bridge, on the corner by the parapet.

The midday sun cast a garish light on the empty square around her. It lit up her face and wrapped itself around her body. She was thirty years old.

This body of hers must keep going, she would force it to, she would not be beaten by it. She would push it hard to get through the fifteen minutes which stood between her and her meeting. She would take the more dangerous short cuts rather than this street, which led straight down to the river.

A few steps further on, the street spun and turned grey. All at once the air seemed to solidify and slabs of plaster obscured the sky.

All M.'s movements slowed to a standstill; her senses were failing. The urgent need to get within sight of the bridge was the one thing that still obsessed her. She refused to collapse.

She hoped that by stretching out her arms, holding her hands straight in front of her, her body would be dragged along, for it was now getting heavier and heavier and her legs had filled with cotton wool.

The fear that she would not get there on time bore into her more deeply than the bullet hole.

How can you define the borders of this country? Why give it a name, why give this woman a name? So many places, so many victims, suffer the same fate.

In the mud where there are paddy fields, on the tarmac where there are cities, because of the lethargy where there are deserts, they are penned into crowds to be beaten and killed or else they die alone: the massacred, the refugees, the martyred and the tortured on every continent have gathered in this street, in this person, in

M., who, all of a sudden, has become the one and only victim. This living, this dying, person.

One act of violence tops another, atrocity follows atrocity, there are faces covered in blood, faces drained of blood; blood pours from men, women, children . . .

It doesn't matter where! The whole of humanity is implicated and the march past is never ending.

Each time one human being is shot, each and every human being cries out in pain. Each and every human being falls into the same abyss, hurled down by the same blind forces.

M. has overestimated her strength. As she looks around for help, her eyes fall on emptiness. She drags herself over to the wall; her groping hands rub up against it and cling to the rough edges. She is still fighting, struggling, shaking her head and battling for breath; but her weakened knees give way, buckle and drag her down to the ground.

M. cries out, but her voice, which coils and tangles in her throat, dwindles to a murmur, which barely skims her lips and dies away. Her forehead is feverish.

Then for a second time a violent pain runs her through. A warm tide oozes from between her shoulder blades and sticks to her blouse.

The young woman finally decides not to fight her body but to lead it on. Trying not to jolt them, she pilots her flesh and bones as they swirl and spin. She makes no attempt to stop her head lolling about or her arms flailing as they fly up, beating the air, searching for somewhere to rest. Taking shallow breaths in the hope of living on until someone walks past who can be trusted with her message, M. lets her body move her around, without losing her real self from sight.

M. tries one position and then another, turning this way and that, bending, swivelling round carefully and deliberately like the slow motion sequences in the films. Then she surrenders to the pull of the ground, to the clumsy fall that gradually brings her down to the pavement where she finds herself curled up like a foetus.

With one cheek pressed to the ground and her eyes wide open, the young woman clings to the last glimmers of consciousness. She is scared at how quickly time is passing and panics when the sun suddenly disappears behind a cloud. But the playful sphere is back again already and her relief when she sees it is plain.

Not far away, a window has started to squeak. The smell of coffee wafts round her.

M. chases away the memories which wash over her. All she wants is the present moment and this fragment of the future, which she is still trying to save. Cautiously, so cautiously, she manages to take from her pocket a postcard-sized colour photograph and a stub of pencil. On the back, at the bottom of a short note, she laboriously scrawls three words.

She knows she will soon be dead. So soon, just when 'living' had still been a possibility.

Death is hovering over this tiny piece of land which is all her own and which is getting smaller by the minute. She remembers the hawk which would hang motionless above one particular district in Cairo, her warm-hearted native city. Slung between its wide tawny wings the predator would dive down towards its prey and suddenly, without wavering, plummet onto the scrap of meat which she had only just put out on the edge of the balcony.

Now, to her left, a few metres ahead of her, the door across a carriage entrance has just this minute opened. Before venturing out into the street, an elderly couple check the roofs where snipers often perch.

They are leaving this dangerous district for good. The man is carrying a suitcase hastily tied up with string. Even before they are quite outside, while they are still on the doorstep, the old couple hold out their hands towards each other and link fingers.

M. pins her eyes on them. M. nestles in the palms of their two hands clasped so affectionately together. Like the old woman, she rests her head on her companion's shoulder and shares the same kiss on her hair.

From deep within her silence, M. calls out to them in despair. She tries, and fails, to move, to attract their attention.

Why did she put on this grey dress, which is lost against the stonework? She should have put on the yellow dress to run off, happy and confident, to her romantic rendezvous.

The old couple are talking quietly to each other.

Then, without seeing her, they set off, in the opposite direction.

As she walks away, the old woman turns round one last time towards her abandoned home.

'When everything's over, we'll come back,' says the man.

She doesn't believe it. She can't believe it any more.

Suddenly she spots a figure, rolled up in a ball on the pavement, and it is moving: 'Look over there.'

They start to make their way back.

Leaning on each other for support, they retrace their steps and cross the roadway as quickly as their legs will carry them.

The old man kneels down and studies the injured woman. He realises that it is serious, that she cannot survive. He has no more revulsion, no more 'whys?' left in him. His eyes fill with rage and tears; and all the time his wife, still on her feet, is shouting, knocking on doors and trying to rouse the neighbours.

No reply. Most of the blocks of flats are empty; their occupants have fled to the mountains. After those few bursts of gunfire, the rest of the population have gone to ground, deep in their shelters.

With a superhuman effort, M. lifts her hand and holds the photograph out to them in her trembling fingers.

The old man takes it, looks at it, turns it over; he tries to make out the note written in blue ink.

'I can't really see, I can't make out what it says. You read it.'

The old woman pulls her silver-rimmed spectacles out of a case hanging round her neck, puts them on and starts to read aloud.

M.'s face appears to relax. She hears the woman say: 'I'll deal with it!'

'By yourself?'

'You can see she can't be left.'

The man agrees. He stares after his wife as she trots briskly off, elbows clamped to her sides, up the street, wide open to attack.

Her husband shields her with his gaze as she grows smaller and smaller in the distance. He still finds her impetuous, tenacious as ever; he can see her as she was at the same age as the dying woman. There was that dim and distant day when, to get over to him on the other side of the avenue, she had launched herself into the crowd and run toward him, braving all the dangers, getting bigger and bigger as she got nearer, working the cars like a bullfighter, her cheeks on fire and her hair a mess. Reckless as ever!

About five hundred metres away, leaning on the parapet of the main bridge, the young man had grown tired of waiting.

Two days before, he had found out M.'s address. He knew that his message and his photograph had reached her. In the last few days the town seemed to have quietened down; the truce was lasting longer than usual.

M. was punctual to a fault; if she had not come it was because she had not wanted to. He had waited too long. All hope had gone.

Because of the royal-blue sweater, the same one he was wearing in the photograph, the old woman recognised him from a long way off. Waving the photograph in the air, she tried to signal to him, to call him over to her.

But a crowded bus hooted behind her so loudly that she hurled herself onto the pavement to let it go by. The huge vehicle swept past her and carried on, hooting louder and louder and jolting from side to side.

Then she saw the young man grab hold of a hand held out from the side of the bus; he hoisted himself up onto the running board before disappearing inside.

She shouted out, but it was no good. The throbbing of the engine drowned her voice. A few seconds later, the bus vanished in a cloud of dust thrown up by its colossal tyres.

Dashed, the old woman leant against the parapet. She waited a few minutes to get her breath back, then she re-read the note.

Each word tore from her a shred of her own youth. Shuddering at the thought that the man who was being carried away, in complete ignorance, could have been her own companion, she could think of only one thing:

getting back to him at once before anything dreadful happened.

She ran back the way she had come, muttering the words written on the back of the photograph which she had, without realising it, learnt by heart:

'We've seen destruction, horrors and hatred in every possible shape and form in our country. Who can we believe in now, what can we believe in? Ever since I've seen death staring me in the face, everything, apart from real love, seems pointless, absurd. From now on, nothing else exists as far as I'm concerned. We love each other, M., no matter what might have happened; let's not stay apart any longer. I'll wait for you tomorrow afternoon, at twelve fifteen, at the corner of the main bridge, like the first time (six years ago already!). A friend is going deliver this note to you; I'll be able to check it's reached you. I'll wear the blue sweater you gave me, the one in this photo. You'll be able to see me a long way off. If you haven't come in an hour, I'll understand that everything is off for good.'

Right at the bottom, the young woman had written her reply in unsteady lettering: 'I was coming . . .'

The old woman knelt down beside her elderly husband, slipped her arm round his shoulders and told him how she had failed to talk to the man. She added: 'One day we'll find him. He's got to know.'

In his turn, the old man told her, in a whisper, that a passer-by had gone off to fetch an ambulance. But he had known all along that there was no hope of saving the young woman.

There was no longer any sign of movement and she was barely breathing. The old woman bent over, let her warm breath sweep across the pale cheek and brushed the forehead with her lips. Then, so carefully, she pulled back the woman's hair and uncovered her ear: taking care with each syllable, she slowly poured out one word after the other to tell her: 'He was waiting for you, at the corner of the main bridge. I saw him, my dear! He was wearing the blue sweater like in your photo. I recognised him immediately. We spoke to each other.'

The sigh, the smile from M. helped her to go on: 'He's on his way. He's coming.'

She turned towards her husband and they exchanged a knowing look. He took over from her: 'He's at the end of the street, he's coming down this way.'

The old woman went on: 'There he is, he's coming!'

'He's getting nearer, here he comes,' he echoed.

'Here he is!'

One voice emphasises the other, twists and turns round the other.

Peace and calm surge thorough the young woman's veins. A wave of happiness spreads across her face. They hear a sigh deeper than one from the deepest seas.

Pleasure and pain take a hold of the old couple. The nonsense and the sense of things jostle in their heads and in their hearts.

Their hands reach out for each other and meet to form one.

This one hand, which has just closed, like a mantle of love, around the lifeless young hand.

The young hand, which is not yet completely cold.

Dinner with the In-Laws

'Who will give me someone to understand me?'
The Book of Job

Once upon a time I was a bookseller; then a long illness prevented me taking any work at all. Nowadays I have a job as a pharmaceutical products rep: I don't make much of a living. I travel back and forward, lugging a case full of samples. My worries never quite get me down completely; I've got a little swing-boat dangling from my heart which means that, in no time at all, I can soar up, away from everything, and feel free again.

We live, my son and I, in a town on the edge of the Mediterranean; it's noisy, overcrowded and glistens silver in the sun whenever there's some of our sporadic but drenching rain. Sounds, colours and opinions clash; I take great delight in the resultant hullabaloo.

The other morning, as I was strolling along with my case, the greengrocer's window bounced my reflection back at me. Antoine wasn't far wrong, my hair was too long. 'You look like an artist!' he'd said to me, a hint of scorn in his voice.

Antoine, my son, is an earnest young man. He has his future all mapped out; he's so exceptionally bright that, after giving him promotion to under-manager, his banker boss is going to give him his daughter. How did I manage to turn out such a successful child? I go through life with my feet on the ground and my mind elsewhere, whereas Antoine forges on indomitably, slowly but surely.

When he was a kid, I was someone who counted for Antoine. My height, I suppose, impressed him. He copied my every move. He used to climb up on my shoulders and call me his 'mountain'. Even though he never got to be as tall as me, now I probably just remind him of a gangling wading bird. These days, when I speak, he doesn't listen: when he speaks, I listen. As far as he's concerned, the horizon can be reached, feelings can be measured and life's a game with a strictly limited number of permutations. As far as I am concerned, the more I learn, the more I'm staggered by my ignorance, the more I look at life, the less I see. His self-confidence would annihilate mine – if I had any!

Antoine was right: hair growing down your neck makes you look odd. I immediately made up my mind to get it trimmed. The next day my son was going to introduce me to his future in-laws – he'd been reluctant to do so until then – and the last thing I wanted to do was embarrass him. So I went into the first barber's I came to.

*

Inside there were four barbers and not a single customer. The owner bellowed out a greeting designed to shake the other three out of their lethargy. In a twinkling, I felt myself being more or less hoisted into the swivel chair. My shoulders were covered with a white cloth whilst a second one was draped round my neck like a bib; the scissors immediately started to snap.

'You'll be wanting quite a lot off, won't you,' said the owner, a fat, kindly man with a waxed moustache.

He thereupon complimented me on the thickness of my hair.

'A lot of youngsters would love to have what you've got.'

And immediately my thoughts turned, forlornly, to Antoine's premature baldness.

'You'll have a coffee with me, won't you,' he suggested a bit later as one of his assistants came in carrying two piping hot cups on a tin tray.

As we chatted we slowly sipped our coffee. He had, apparently, travelled far and wide; I started in on a whole load of questions which he answered, obviously pleased to be asked. But as soon as he picked up his scissors again, I realised that he needed silence. So, leaving my head in the capable hands of this affable man, I buried myself in the pile of newspapers that had been discreetly placed on my knees.

Still feeling quite disturbed by the news item I had just read – a child had been battered by his stepmother and then shut up for a week in an attic – I neglected to look in the mirror when he had finished cutting.

'What do I owe you?'

'Whatever you want.'

Prices in our country vary according to how well you get on with each other, the occasion or the time of day; being naturally diffident, I cope very badly with this apparent freedom.

'But you . . .'

'Don't let that come between us,' replied the man, adding to my embarrassment.

He must have seen the look of dismay on my face, for my new friend took pity on me and suggested a sum which seemed to me extremely low. However, I didn't dare dither longer. I was particularly touched because I seemed to have been the only customer of the morning. So I asked him to add the price of the two coffees to the bill. That was when he got indignant: 'Now you have offended me! You come into my shop for the first time, we chat like long-lost friends and now you are asking me the price of my coffee.'

Mortified, I thanked him and, shaking his hand, promised to come back.

'My shop is all yours,' he said as he walked me to the door.

The bank where my son worked was a few doors down from the barber's and, as good luck would have it, I met Antoine on my way out.

As soon as he saw me, he yelped: 'What have they done to your hair! Good grief, it's terrible. You look like a convict.'

I could see by his face that going to the dinner with the fiancée's family was now out of the question and that Antoine was already searching for a plausible reason to explain my absence. He then scuttled off, looking back over his shoulder two or three times to make sure I wasn't following him.

My legs turned to lead. I wanted to sink to the ground and wait for a child – a child like my Antoine when he was little – to put his hand in mine and help me up.

Someone was shouting to me: 'Here, you forgot this.'

It was the barber who, delighted at having found me, was holding up my case. His friendly slap on the back brought me back to life.

'I'm on my own,' I told him. 'Shall we eat together?'

I pointed to the café-restaurant opposite where the tables spilled out onto the pavement. He agreed: 'Give me a moment to close the shop and I'll be with you.'

I crossed the road. I was hot; the sun, glowering over the town, wrapped itself round my skull, no longer protected by its mane of hair.

From where I was sitting I could see the bank and also my new friend's shop.

As I waited, my gaze shifted several times from one to the other. And, very gently, the swing-boat swung upwards.

Born of the Shadows

For Richard Rognet

Waking at the edge of night to catch the dawn. Lying in wait for the hint of amber which, any minute now, will tinge the façade opposite, highlighted by its four windows and their off-white, half-open shutters.

Greeting these budding, timid rays which fan out, so, so slowly, from an unchanging horizon; a horizon shrouded by the stony tapestry of the urban landscape.

Living in a narrow city street, every morning, from my bed I witness the sun's first conjuring tricks on the wall outside. I spot, on grey shadows lingering on the stucco, a sliver of twilight which will slowly but surely give way to the dazzling light of day.

At this time in the morning, you don't see a soul. Not even a shadow behind the opaque net curtains.

Imprisoned within my own window frame, I watch the fleeting patch on the small building which lies before me. I scrutinise this narrow, confined surface. It becomes a screen on which, soon, the course of the sun and the hurley-burley of life will unfold.

Depending on the weather and the seasons, this roughcast wall will be covered in all the nuances, all the subtleties of daybreak. The frail, ethereal arrival of morning on the brink of resurrection.

Slowly, life will establish itself once more.

Born of the shadows, this infallible, faithful, diurnal light will soon coat my portion of wall. It will bounce from the windows, adorn the gables, burnish the gutters, steal across the ochre tiles and melt into the blue-tinged tarns as they emerge, inch by inch, from the fabric of the night.

All these half-tones are washed with colour: the slats of the shutters turn unquestionably white, the windows gleam, the lead of the guttering brightens as it waits for the usual tribe of clumsy-footed pigeons.

Within a few minutes the surroundings are all aglow.

Here, proof of the coming day, pulled from the tangled weeds and the terrors of the dark, comes light.

Behind the suddenly translucent nets, bodies stir. I glimpse a man's torso. I identify a child's arm, the silhouette of an old man. A woman's hands push open the shutters. I concoct a story to fit them – light years, no doubt, from the truth.

Artlessly the light hesitates a moment before tugging

the hours, gradually, from tint to tint, toward the heralded radiance of noon.

Born of the shadows, the light asserts itself, dominates, turns lord and master.

Then, faithful to the solar cycle, it wanes and crumbles away before succumbing to the night.

Dependable, nonetheless, like hope, light withers to dawn anew, all the brighter, in ever-fresh and familiar arcs of cloudless sky.

Between the Worlds

I'm back from one of my strolls through Paris and I'm in a good mood; my affection for my city, my intimacy with it, have never ceased to delight me.

My letter to Annie, which I have just stuffed into my jeans' pocket, is worrying me less and less. I can visualise quite clearly now what I have to say to her. I've already jotted down a few lines. Now I'm home, I'll finish off the note.

As I was sitting at the pavement café where I had started to write to her, my decision had flashed before me as clearly as the autumn sun, which was warming the metal-bound disk of marble on which my notepaper rested.

Being at a table like that, surrounded by the city – enjoying my cappuccino and my croissant, letting my eyes flit over the never-ending variety of passers-by – always puts me in good spirits which clear my head and my heart.

I'll start my letter: 'Annette, sweetie-pie, poppet . . .' No, I'll say: 'Anne, my dearest . . .' We were at a turning point in our lives which required a certain seriousness, a certain gravitas. I'll sign it: 'Paul' and not the usual 'Paulo'.

Annie just loves diminutives and silly names. When she uses them I have to suppress a slight feeling of irritation; then I give in to these little quirks which give her so much pleasure. By an odd paradox, Annie also thoroughly enjoys grandiloquence: words which puff up and grow breathless. That's when I really have trouble not showing my exasperation. But, more often than not, as I'm determined to avoid souring our lives in those pointless arguments which embitter ageing couples, I gloss over such trifles.

In these circumstances – as in others, for example, where I'm trapped in a formal dinner or at a cocktail party – a satisfying mist floats up into my head. I barely hear what is being said around me; I drift away, I settle elsewhere, I go to some inner place, immune from all irritation!

Being of Mediterranean stock, I had more than my fill, as a child, of flailing arms, wild words and violent rages, all of which were immediately swept away beneath sweetness and light. Constantly surrounded by purple faces, glowering eyes and mouths which spat curses promptly followed by a blessing and a kiss, I would tremble and take refuge in Sophia's skirts. My mother seemed to be as terrified of these excesses as I was.

Having witnessed the formidable energy expended just to squash a fly, even today, as an adult, I have a deep-rooted allergy to such screaming, such swaggering, such swearing as you would expect to find only in the pages of Aeschylus or Euripides! It was then I felt the need to be off, to escape to the ends of the earth, to identify with northern peoples. Or, just as happily, to wander, all alone, through vast and silent lands.

Annie, despite being a daughter of the North, assures me that she married me mainly because of my impetuous, sun-drenched heritage. It is this, so she says, that has endowed me with a way of shaking a hand, of bestowing a friendly peck on the cheek, of giving a hug, of extending a warm invitation, of juggling with metaphors, of joking, of bursting into laughter, and that attracted her from the start.

The coldness, the self-control of her race inhibit, she adds, dreams and desires. Avoiding excess, thinking before speaking, being in control of their gestures, toning down any hint of spontaneity, have drained the colour from their cheeks and glazed their eyes. What's more, she claims, overly repressed instincts burst out unexpectedly and can never be curbed. It's at that point they break all bounds, degenerate into all sorts of excesses, explode in acts of violence and despair which go well beyond ours.

'I don't care what you do, I don't care what you say,' Anne concludes, 'despite your newly acquired self-possession you're still full of visions and feelings. You're an odd concoction!'

I snap back: 'Odd concoction yourself!'

Annie calls me her 'rising sun'. To encourage me, she quotes as role models the achievements, financial and professional, of several members of my family scattered across the globe. She seems to think they are better examples to motivate me than her own sedentary family, firmly ensconced in its own perpetual twilight. Her people work in such poorly publicised, poorly paid fields as philology, botany and philosophy and shun the world of conquering heroes.

In many respects I would have loved to join them in their uncomplicated lives. But Annie wants me to be a success: 'Tortured artists are a thing of the past, gone for good. Anyway, you've made a name for yourself. You're certainly no tortured artist.'

'Anne, my darling . . .' The words dance on my paper. I can see them emerging letter by letter, clearly legible on the shiny paper.

Under the circumstances, I won't use the electronic typewriter which Annie gave me. And yet I feel an almost divine pleasure whenever I run my fingers over its dull brown keys. I barely touch them and, behold, lines wing their way onto the paper in a deliciously whispered hiss. What goes on in the entrails of machines is a true miracle; a miracle I am too ignorant or too lazy to attempt to decipher. As in a fairy-tale garden which dumbfounds the visitor time after time with ever more astounding fruit, I'm fascinated by new technology.

But what I want to express this morning is too inti-mately part of me, part of Annie, part of our years together for me to be able to confide the writing of it to an intermediary – albeit one as agreeable, as faithful as my machine. To write what I have to write, I need my whole hand. I need to feel my fingers grasp the black felt-tip pen from which the ink must flow freely.

Swept along by the pumping of my blood, by the throbbing of my arteries, my love will be set down in each symbol, my affection engraved in each loop and flourish. That way, my words will cause less damage.

'Anne, my darling . . .'

My hand scurries from one paragraph to the next; then hesitates, backtracks, crosses out; and is off again.

Suddenly the sight of this hand disconcerts me. In my mind's eye I see it linked to Annie's, surmounting obstacles, outdistancing the years. Could I do without this bond? The thought of a permanent break engulfs me, destroying the translucence of the day.

We had met, Annie and I, aged sixteen, on one of my country's baking hot beaches. By a strange twist of fate, only a few months later we met up again in the snow and wind of hers. Ever since, our climates and our temperaments have worked in unison; or have clashed in conflicting, invigorating interplay.

Our rows – frequent, passionate, but short-lived – heed the appeal of our hands and melt away. One hand grasps the other; and unravels, in this one gesture, all our bad times. As we reached our fifties, the same phenomenon was still happening.

In the cinema – we go regularly, without fail – surrounded by the darkness, we never know who's going to make the first move. It's like a game which combines affection and flirtation. The initiative is the prerogative of neither one. Our eyes – in perfect unison thanks to our shared passion for films – remain fixed on the screen, whilst the hand of one slips, stealthily, toward the knee, then the elbow, then the forearm, then the wrist of the other.

This then, despite the disagreements and the irritations, sets the seal, mysteriously, once more on our love. As our palms meet, as our fingers intertwine, the rough edges of everyday life disappear.

Faced with an announcement as important as today's, I ought to start my letter with: 'Dear Anne . . .'

No! It's a turn of phrase I find repulsive. The ardent suns of my childhood, the rebelliousness of Sophia, my mother, stir in my blood and force me to reject such a cold, distant expression. Nor can I get used to the forms of address which start and end business letters. I find it impossible to communicate, however briefly, with someone who takes refuge behind an adopted persona. At the risk of shocking my correspondent, I always start and end my letters as I see fit.

Despite what my letter will be saying, Anne will always be: 'My darling, my one and only, my Annie . . .' Nowadays, at a time when it's the done thing to be a serial adulterer, to have affair after affair, I do believe I can claim – taking into consideration one or two entanglements which left no lasting scars – that we loved each other, Annie and I, more or less continuously.

How can it be that after thirty years of living together I am ready to leave her, and for another love?

'Anne, my darling, from now on, my life will be spent far from you.'

I can already make out her questions: 'Who will you be with? You must tell me, Paul.'

I can hear myself replying: 'I don't want to hide anything from you.'

Anne is beside herself: 'Do I know her?'

'Of course.'

'How can you say "of course" just like that? How long have you known her?'

'For ever.'

'Before us?'

'Yes, before us.'

'We were only sixteen when we first met!'

'Well, I was ten when it happened and I have been in love ever since.'

'So all these years, you've been hiding something. You've been lying to me, for thirty years?'

Anne is panicking, beginning to shout. She asks menacingly: 'Who is it?'

We arrived at the Gare de Lyon in Paris, my mother Sophia and I.

It was 1948. The Second World War had only just ended. Shoulders back, which showed off her fine bust, and head held high, my mother appeared, thanks to her bearing, much more imposing than she really was.

The day before our escape she had undone her plaits, cut

her long black hair and adopted a short, wavy hairstyle. I had always been struck by her passionate, silent mouth and the intense green of her eyes. Very soon I had learnt to read her expressive gaze; to make out, in its depths, forceful but suppressed meaning. A meaning which nothing had managed to stifle. Nothing. Not even my father's severity when, as soon as she opened her mouth, he ordered Sophia not to interrupt him; not even the strangle-hold maintained by the family and which curbed her fledgling ideas and put a check on her imagination.

I was barely ten when Sophia left home, with me in tow. There was never any question of our being apart. And then one June morning there we were, the two of us, in the middle of Paris.

Her heart was pounding and I thought I could hear each throb. Suddenly my mother dropped to her knees on the pavement. I can still see the huge clock, as grey as the sky, looming over us. I remember the look of amazement on the faces of the dark-skinned porter and a group of passengers. Sophia put her arms round me and hugged me to her breast:

'Free! Free, Paulo! We're in freedom-city. You must love it. You must always be free . . . Are you happy?'

I nodded as I helped her up. At first it was her joy which made me happy. Then, almost immediately, it was my own. And soon, as I got to know the city, I fell forever in love with it.

*

'At this turning point in our lives, as the time we have left to live slips away, I have chosen to stay with the one I love, my dear little Anne. I can't abandon this mistress which means everything to me, my past, my present, my future. She gives me life without my having to move an inch. She has had so much to contend with, she has suffered so much; she has exercised power, she has been enslaved. She embraces so many flights of fancy, so many faces. She has wide-open spaces and mysterious corners. I chart her every nook and cranny, and lose myself in them without ever getting lost. Her shadows quiz me, her lights revive me.'

'You're mad, Paulo! You only get that in books! Keep your cloud-cuckoo land for your paintings, I don't want it!'

Despite the ravages of age, Anne is still beautiful. Yet in spite of all her diets, her exercises, her air of defiance when you suggest she slow down a little, I can still see that her legs are stiffening up, that her hips and her back are less flexible. But, all things considered, she's still young, lively, energetic. Unruffled by time zones and changes in climate; she's brave, bold, always ready to take control.

These past two years Annie has been dashing around, for her firm, all five continents. At their request she is going to take up a post overseas, very soon.

'That's where it'll all be happening, from now on.'

Anne travels by road, rail and air without worrying about losing her bearings or being tired. I do admire her, but the mere thought of all this coming and going, of being caught up in her hectic lifestyle, makes my head spin. If I took the plunge and stayed with her I get the feeling that my studio would go to rack and ruin, that my colours would fade the minute they touched the canvas, that they would drip from the stretcher, splashing my clothes, the easel, the floor. Mastery over my hands and my thoughts would elude me. I would find myself spattered with paint, my hands dangling idly at my sides; in utter confusion, in utter chaos.

'You'll never be a winner, Paulo. You're marking time while I'm moving on. What is this strange love you're sacrificing me for?'

'And what about you?'

I've given up these pointless confrontations which leave us battered and at odds with each other. Nor do I try to argue in order to hold on to Annie. Her freedom is as important to me as mine; and Sophia's voice, despite her death so few years after our arrival in Paris, still haunts me: 'Free, Paulo! Free and happy!'

Once upon a time, I found I had a problem with jealousy. Was it a legacy of my Mediterranean heritage? I don't really think that true love can be free of it. Time has smoothed away the sharp edges of the one and healed the wounds or the other. I'm all the better for that. I am positive, however, that I still love Annie; the only difference is that distance, and all she keeps secret, no longer worry me.

*

I pick up the telephone; my wife is ringing from far, far away. I can feel she's under pressure. She's just rented a tiny apartment in a town ideally placed for her business trips. She probably wants me to be with her: 'I've guessed your mysterious mistress. You're a bit behind the times, Paulo. You're doing a Josephine Baker: '*J'ai deux amours*, my Annie and Paris . . .'

I suggest a date when I think I will have finished the three paintings I'm working on at the moment. Anne replies, irritably: 'That week I'll be in Korea, I've already told you!'

I quickly rifle through the little pad I keep in my pocket where I note down her movements, meeting after meeting, contact number after contact number.

'You're right. I'm sorry. Just at the moment, I don't think . . . I'll write.'

'You'll write? You're joking, Paulo. You're lucky being an artist. Do you think I've got time to read a letter? Let alone answer one!'

Suddenly I'm angry: 'Listen, Annie, I've made up my mind, I'm . . .'

She's hung up.

I crumple up my letter then tear it to shreds. Gradually I pull myself together and decide to wander my city until evening.

I walk down the rue de Seine, cross the rue de Buci. The market, the colours, the stalls, the quips from the traders put me back in a good mood. I wander down to the embankments, zigzagging between the road and the edge of the narrow pavement. The passing cars hum in background; the noise follows in my wake but doesn't disturb me.

I stroll across the pont des Arts. I stop. I watch the passers-by – those from here, those from elsewhere. I stare at the bustling banks of the river. I marvel at the pink-tinged buildings steeped in history and the vagaries of time. I peer down over the parapet and the powerful flow of the Seine. I start – as did Sophia and her captive tongue – a silent conversation with the river. I set rapidly off again.

I amble along to see how the building work in the courtyard of the Louvre is progressing; I visualise what it's going to look like. I retrace my steps and go over the pont Henri IV. I indulge myself in nudging each of the massive doors all along the rue Christine and the rue Suger. Each time one opens a crack, I glimpse a façade, a passageway, a courtyard, a tiny garden.

By nightfall I have reached Montparnasse Cemetery. I walk in. I saunter up and down the paths looking for the little plot of city ground which, by some miracle, I have managed to acquire.

'Are you happy?' Sophia asks.

I am happy! Sometimes it's as simple as that. An effervescent glee takes hold of my very being, obliterating age, sadness, anxiety. Wrapped in the cocoon of this city, I am reborn.

*

My career's not going well; this often irritates Annie. But my painting allows me to live and take things easy. I have friends and, for my very own use, time I do not have to account for, time for dreaming.

'You will be free and happy, my pet,' insists Sophia, whose passion is bursting in my veins.

I love happiness, Sophia. You gave me the taste for it. I can make it come to life, out of nothing, out of everything! I'm happy despite this body of mine which is slowly undermining me. Despite this often painful tussle with my canvases. Despite bereavement and heartache. Despite and thanks to Annie.

Little by little, the image of my love revives.

Our hands stretch toward each other; they will entwine once more.

Tomorrow, Annie will call me by telephone.

Or, I'll call Annie.

Those Violets

For Marie-Ange Underwood

To thank me for a favour, and spot on my birthday (just how had she found out the crucial date?), Juanita gave me a little pot of violets, wrapped up in cellophane and topped off with a silvery bow.

My words of thanks stuck in my throat.

Flowers of every kind I adore. On the other hand, I nurse a permanent, deep-rooted aversion to houseplants.

I've seen so many: they take over, they sprout here, there and everywhere, they wind themselves round each other, they flourish as if they were growing in the forests of the Amazon, they climb up banisters, wrap themselves round handrails, cling to bookshelves, worm their way into every corner and fan out in front of windows, cutting off the light of day.

They're exacting and possessive. They demand jugs of water, canes, fertiliser pellets and supports. I've seen their owners ensnared in all this growth. I've seen them gradually bewitched by each new shoot, gradually captivated by each young tendril.

Of course that could never be true of violets – neat,

modest little plants that they are. But for me, in their own small way, the ones Juanita had given me suddenly became almost the classic example of a despotic, rampant plant world in my own home.

Such a broad smile spread across Juanita's face that I smiled back; despite everything I was touched by the elegance and the thoughtfulness of her gesture.

My smile elicited: 'Violets can live a very long time and flower several times a year.'

I shuddered at the thought of it. She went on: 'You just have to look after them.'

To make sure I wasn't going to neglect them she immediately handed me a bag of soil and some plant-food granules, explaining in great detail what the flowers needed in the way of water, light and shade.

At last Juanita went blithely off, leaving me with a predicament.

It would be impossible to get rid of the violets straight away; I couldn't give them, for example, to my neighbours along the hall who took great delight in their rampant indoor garden. Juanita used to come once a week to do my housework; her probing eyes would notice immediately if the plant was missing. I wouldn't have wanted to upset her for the world.

There we were, face to face: the violets and me.

There was no way round it, I just could not appreciate their feel, their smell or their colour.

Violets. Their stems barely raise the blooms above the mass of tightly packed, greyish leaves which look almost as if they are covered with a thin dusting of mildew. Within its compact shape, this plant encompasses all the sorrows of the world. Wrinkled, matted and dour, it makes me think of certain women, whingers even in their first flush of youth, old at heart before their time. Their twisted, misguided sensitivities (which can, at times, make them quite alluring) make them see themselves as constantly neglected victims. They find their only comfort in real or imaginary ailments and undiagnosable illnesses.

That's the way violets strike me, I can't help it: they make the most out of their weaknesses and are inveterate convalescents!

Although it's the result of mixing blue and red – brisk, lively colours – their colouring and their appearance make me think of some pallid, funereal emblem, the personification of all that is melancholy.

Whenever I see them, I feel this wild longing for fiery poppies, tousled peonies, shimmering dahlias, bold tulips! I am consumed by the craving to douse all this mauve and all this purple in thick layers of sunshine. So I conjure up in my mind's eye the flowers of springtime: primroses from the fields and the woods, nasturtiums, daffodils, broom – despite its thorns – and above all those bewitching sunflowers Van Gogh so loved!

To me, the scent of violets, supposedly delicate and fragrant, seems lifeless and dull. It reminds me of the sickly-sweet smell of dried flowers; of that hint of mustiness which dilapidated linen chests, memorials to successive generations, give off as soon as you open them.

In short, everything about this flower discourages and depresses me. It has no plumage, no heart, no autonomy!

When Juanita had gone, I set my plant free of the layer of foil wrapped round the pot. Stripped bare, the porous, terracotta clay will allow the little lump of earth to breathe.

Once I had got them – and even though they didn't arouse the slighted scrap of feeling in me – I looked after my violets conscientiously.

Buried deep within them, there was something alive! There was something growing and struggling to survive, to exist.

I watered my plant faithfully. I gave it the approved amount of light and shade. I picked off the dead shoots. Over the soil I scattered the white powder that Juanita had recommended.

After a year of painstaking care I do believe I had become quite fond of it.

And yet, when the summer holidays came, off I went, forgetting to put the plant and its flowers out of harm's way. I left them on a south-facing sill beneath the louvred window in my kitchen.

I remembered them only once I was on the train.

Overcome with remorse, I tried phoning first my neigh-
bours then some obliging friends as soon as I arrived. It
was the middle of August. There was no one still in Paris.

For the first few hours, whenever I thought about the
poor innocents cruelly exposed to the heat of the
summer sun, and all because of my carelessness, I felt
quite upset.

Then I forgot all about them . . .

The mountains were cool and welcoming.

I came back every evening from our long rambles with
my arms full of wild herbs and meadow flowers.

My violets slipped from my mind. They faded further
and further from my mind.

In September I got back laden with heavy bags and
glowing good health. It was only when I had closed the
landing door that, all of a sudden, I remembered my
violets. I dashed into the kitchen.

A pitiful sight met my eyes!

My plant had been reduced to a brittle shell; dusty
green in colour, withered, curled up like a fist. All I
could see were shrivelled petals and wizened leaves.
From it rose the faint, fetid smell of drains.

My embarrassment and my remorse were supplanted
by a feeling of disgust. And yet I wasn't in a hurry to get
rid of it and to throw it in the kitchen bin.

To me, this plant, having lived however briefly,
seemed to have been blessed and dignified by its tran-

sient gift of life. No, it would not go out with the rubbish! I would sooner drown it in the river or bury it in the earth.

In an attempt to show it sympathy and kindness, I took the pot of violets in my hands. The thin earth crumbled. My flowers were now a mere jumble of roots and rough stems.

Then, suddenly, in the midst of the catastrophe, at the very core of the devastation, I thought I caught sight of the tiniest speck of green.

I could not believe my eyes; I put on my glasses. I was right. There it was: a minute leaf struggling amidst the ruins and the debris.

I gave a whoop of triumph. Then, quick as I could, I plunged my plant into a bowl of tepid water so that the moisture could gently soak through the pores of the clay pot, then gave its sick, hardened soil a dusting of fertiliser.

Every hour on the hour I peered at it. I talked to it endlessly.

Within three days my violets had revived.

That was when I started taking an almost maternal delight in watching their progress.

For three good years we rubbed along, my plant and I: through winter and back to spring, through death and back to life.

In the end I came to delight in its velvety leaves; to be charmed by its purplish tones, to be won over by its graceful modesty.

Then one day, their time came. My violets ceased to live.

Like those who have reached a very great age, who have lived to the full the blessing of a long life, my flowers made a good death, leaving me feeling calm and fulfilled.

On my way to the office, I pass the marché aux Fleurs every day.

There are flowers everywhere, on the ground, on racks, rack upon rack. I also see, forming their own modest little procession, a row of pots with violets in them. But never would I dream of replacing my dead plant.

On the other hand, depending on the season, I buy armfuls of wallflowers, roses, marguerites, carnations, tulips and fronds. I find the brevity of their lives particularly attractive.

But, welling up somewhere in a corner of my mind, in some hidden niche in my heart, I can sense a lingering, delicate, velvety memory tinged with mauve or deepest purple.

Enduring Patience

'She is like very deep water whose ripples we cannot fathom.'

Vizier Ptahhotep, *Teachings on the Subject of Women*, 2600 BC

Someone was scratching at the door.

Amina put her newest baby on the ground and got up.

Left alone, the baby flew into a fit of rage, whereupon one of his older sisters – half naked and crawling on all fours – made a dash to get to him.

At first the little girl just stood still, fascinated by her younger brother's tiny face, his cheeks, his crimson forehead. Then she dabbed at the fragile eyelids, pressing her forefinger onto one of the child's tears which she put to her lips to taste the salt. Finally she burst out crying, drowning the baby's wailing with her own sobs.

At the far end of the room – a cramped room with earth walls and a low ceiling – which was all there was in the way of living space, two older girls, their dresses in rags, their hair dishevelled and their lips covered in flies, were fighting over the rind of a melon. Samyra, aged seven, armed with a ladle, was chasing the chickens which were running about in every direction. Her younger brother, Osman, was attempting to climb onto the back of the goat which was skittering about.

Exasperated, Amina turned round to her pack of children before opening the door: 'Shut up! If you wake your father, he'll beat the lot of you.'

Her threats went unheeded; of her nine children there was always one or other of them whining or shouting. She shrugged and turned, ready to unbolt the door.

'Who knocked?' asked a sleepy voice. It was Zekr, her husband.

It was the time of day when, in their huts that were no more than blocks of hardened, cracked mud, the men dozed before going back to the fields. As for the women, they never slept.

Amina lifted the hasp off the latch – the fixing had come loose and barely held it onto the wood – and the hinges grated, setting her teeth on edge. How many times had she asked Zekr to oil them? She pulled open the door and let out a cry of delight: 'Osman the Pilgrim!'

Osman the Pilgrim had made the holy journey to Mecca several times. He was renowned for his virtues. For years he had been wandering the countryside, begging for his food and scattering his blessings generously. As he passed, diseases withered and crops grew vigorously once more. Even from afar the villagers recognised his long black robe topped with the drab-coloured woollen muffler which he wore wound round his upper body and his head.

'You bring honour to our house, holy man! Walk in!'

It took just one visit from him for all your wishes to be fulfilled. They said that in Suwef, thanks to the laying on of hands, a boy from the village who had only ever grunted since the day he was born had suddenly started to produce words. Amina had witnessed the miracle of Zeinab, a girl in her early teens, whose frequent fits had terrified her neighbours as she rolled in the sand, her legs flailing and her lips curled back. Osman the Pilgrim had been summoned, he had uttered a few words; and ever since, Zeinab had been free from seizures. There was even talk of finding a husband for her.

Amina opened the door wider. Light flooded into the room: 'Walk in, holy man. My home is your home.'

The man declined, preferring to remain outside: 'Bring me water and bread. I have walked far and my strength has left me.'

Waking with a start, Zekr recognised the voice. He hurriedly put on his skullcap and, seizing the handle of the ewer, got up and set off across the dimly lit room, rubbing his eyes.

As soon as her husband reached the doorstep and greeted the old man, the woman withdrew.

Once the door was closed behind her, Amina went over to her clay oven.

No weariness ever caused her to stoop. She had that indomitable gait of Egyptian peasant women who seem to be constantly carrying the weight of a fragile burden balanced on their heads.

Was she young? Barely thirty! But what is to be made of youth when no one cares for it?

The woman bent over in front of the oven to pull out of a cubbyhole the week's bread rolled up in a hessian cloth. There were still a few dried-out olives in the bottom of a bowl and two rows of onions were hanging on the wall. The woman counted the flat loaves, judged their weight and put them to her cheek to check how fresh they were. Having selected the two best she dusted them off with the back of her hand and blew on them. Then, bearing them like a votive offering on her outspread hands she went once more to the door.

She was thrilled by the presence of the visitor. Her hut seemed less mean, her children less shrill and Zekr's voice more spirited, more alive.

As she walked through the room she bumped into two of her children. One of them clutched at her skirts and reached up to snatch a loaf: 'Me, me. I'm hungry.'

'Go away, Barsoum. It's not for you. Let go!'

'I'm not Barsoum, I'm Ahmed.'

The darkness in the room had shrouded their faces.

'I'm hungry!'

Roughly, she pushed the child aside. He slipped, fell and rolled over on the ground, screaming.

Feeling guilty, she moved on faster, hurriedly opened the door and stepped out. Immediately closing the door behind her, she leant the full weight of her back against it. Her face was in a sweat, her lips were pursed. She stood stock still facing the old man and her husband, gulping in air to fill her lungs.

'The eucalyptus beneath which I used to rest, the one growing in the middle of the oat field . . .' Osman the Pilgrim began.

'. . . is still there,' sighed the woman.

'Last time it looked quite wizened.'

'. . . is still there,' she repeated. 'Nothing here ever changes. Nothing ever changes.'

The words she had just said suddenly made her want to weep, to bemoan her fate. The old man would listen to her; he would reassure her, perhaps. But about what? She did not rightly know. 'About everything,' she thought.

'Take these loaves. They are for you!'

The empty ewer lay on the ground. Osman the Pilgrim took the flat loaves from the woman's hands and thanked her. He slid one of the loaves under his robe so it rested against his chest; he bit into the other. He chewed thoroughly, making each mouthful last.

Amina was flattered when she saw that he was regaining his strength thanks to her bread and a smile returned to her lips. Then, remembering that her husband hated her staying outside the house for long, she took her leave of the two men, her head bowed.

'May Allah shower you with good fortune!' declared the old man. 'May he bless you and grant you seven more children!'

The woman leant against the wall to steady herself, shrank down into her loose black robes and hid her face.

'What's the matter with you? Are you ill?' enquired

the old man.

She was unable to find her words. Finally she stammered out: 'I already have nine children, holy man. I beg of you, take back your blessing.'

He thought he had misunderstood, she was mumbling so badly: 'What did you say? Say it again.'

'Take back your blessing, I beg of you.'

'I do not understand,' interrupted the old man. 'You do not know what you are saying.'

With her face still buried in her hands, the woman shook her head from left to right and from right to left: 'No! No! . . . Enough! . . . Enough is enough.'

All around her children were turning into locusts, swooping down on her, circling round her, reducing her to an inert lump of earth. By their thousands, their hands – now talons, now stinging nettles – were pulling at her robes and tearing at her flesh.

'No, no! I can't go on!'

She was fighting for breath: 'Take back your blessing.'

Zekr, stunned by her audacity, stood in front of her and said not a word.

'Blessings are in God's hands, I can change nothing now.'

'You can . . . you *have to* take it back!'

Osman the Pilgrim looked away, his lips curling scornfully.

But she continued to harry him: 'Take back your blessing! Do what I ask. You have to take back your blessing.'

Clenching her fists she moved toward him: 'You must do what I ask!'

'No. I will not take back a single thing.'

A gleam flashed in her eyes and she moved further forward. Was this the same woman as a few moments ago?

'Take back your blessing,' she screamed.

That look in her eyes, that voice, where had she got them from?

'What will be the use of taming the river? What will be the use of the ripening crops? Before we get them, there will be thousands more mouths to feed! Have you seen our children? What do they look like to you? Have you really looked at them?'

Opening wide the door of her hut, she shouted inside: 'Barsoum, Fatma, Osman, Naghi! Come here. Come here, all of you! You older ones can carry the little ones. Come out, all nine of you. Let's see you!'

'You're mad.'

'Let's see your arms, your shoulders! Pull your dresses up and let's see your stomachs, your legs, your knees!'

'You are rejecting life,' said the old man indignantly.

'Don't talk about life! You know nothing about life.'

'Children bring life!'

'Too many children bring death!'

'Amina! that is blasphemy!'

'I am appealing to God!'

'God is not listening to you.'

'He will listen to me.'

'If I were your husband, I would punish you.'

'Today no one will lift a hand against me. No one!'

She caught hold of the Pilgrim's hand as it swung down towards her.

'Not even you! Take back your blessing or I will never leave hold of you.'

She shook him to make him take back his words: 'Do what I tell you: take back your blessing.'

'You are possessed by demons! Stand away, do not touch me. I am not one to take anything back.'

Although the old man had appealed to him several times, Zekr remained silent and motionless. Then, all of a sudden, he moved. Was he going to set on Amina and beat her, as he so often did?

'You, Zekr, on your knees. It's your turn to try to make him understand. Beg! With me!'

The words spilled out of her! How had she dared utter them and in that commanding tone of voice? Suddenly overcome by a fit of trembling, suffocated by her long history of fear, her fingers slackened, her legs went as limp as cotton. Raising her elbows to shield herself from the blows, she cowered against the wall.

'The woman is right, holy man. Take back your blessing.'

She could not believe her ears. Or her eyes. Zekr had listened to her. There Zekr was, on his knees at the feet of the old man.

*

Hearing the shouts, the neighbours came running from all over. Zekr tried to catch Amina's eye as she knelt next to him; the woman was overwhelmed with gratitude.

'Holy man, take back your blessing,' they begged as one.

A tight circle had formed around them. Convinced that the crowd was on his side, the old man drew himself up onto the tips of his toes and raised a threatening fore-finger: 'This man and this woman reject God's plan. They are sinners! Drive them out lest our village be beset by misfortune.'

'Seven more children! He wished seven more children on us! How will we be able to manage?' groaned Amina.

Fatma, her cousin, already had eight little ones. Soad had six. Fathia, who always had her youngest in tow, the one with the bad teeth and the wild look in her eyes, had four boys and three girls. And the other women? They were all the same! . . . Yet each of these women, fright-ened and uncertain as they were, stared at Amina warily.

'Births are in the hands of God,' pontificated Fatma, looking to the old man and the other men for approval.

'We are the ones who should decide if we want chil-dren,' declared Zekr, suddenly getting up.

'That's blasphemy,' objected Khalifé, a young man with prominent ears. 'Something dreadful will happen to us.'

'Drive them out,' repeated the old man insistently. 'They are desecrating this place.'

Amina placed a sisterly hand on her husband's shoulder.

'You should listen to Osman the Pilgrim, he is a holy man,' muttered some anxious voices.

'No, I am the one you should listen to!' bellowed Zekr. 'I am just like you! It's Amina that you should listen to. Amina is a woman like any other woman. How will she manage with seven more children? How will we manage?'

His cheeks were ablaze. From a distance, someone repeated, like a timid echo: 'How will they manage?'

Passed from mouth to mouth the words grew louder: 'What will they do?'

'No more children!' suddenly shouted out a small blind girl clinging to her mother's skirts.

What had happened to this village, to its inhabitants, to this whole valley? thought Osman the Pilgrim, shaking his head sorrowfully.

'No more children!' went on the voices.

Leaning on his crutches Mahmoud hobbled up on his one leg to the old man and whispered in his ear: 'You can see they have had enough! Take back your blessing.'

'I will not take back a thing.'

Elbowing his way out of the crowd, the holy man called down curses on them, and with an angry gesture jostled the one-legged man who lost his crutches and rolled to the ground.

That was the signal!

*

Fikhry threw himself on the old man.

To avenge the man with one leg, Zekr struck out too.

Salah, lashing the air with his bamboo stick, drew nearer.

There was a whirling and whooping of gestures and shouts. Hoda ran forward with a scrap of hosepipe. A little lad pulled a sharp post out of a fence. A grandmother broke off a branch of weeping willow and waded into the fray.

'No more children!'

'Take back your blessing!'

'We've had enough!'

'We want to live our lives.'

'Live our lives.'

Towards evening, the gendarmes found Osman the Pilgrim face down next to a trampled loaf and a shattered ewer. They picked him up, dusted off his garments and took him to the nearest infirmary.

The next day there was a raid on the village. The men who had taken part in the disturbance were taken off in a grey van. The prison vehicle jolted away along the towpath leading to the police post.

Their eyes glittering, Amina and her companions gathered at the edge of the village and stared for a long time at the route the van had taken.

The clouds of dust lingered on. Their husbands were indeed far, far away . . . but never had they felt so close to them. Never.

That day was unlike any other.

That day had seen the end of their enduring patience.

Here and Now

For Louis Senior

'I'm all for living in the here and now!' Wallace found the expression comforting, especially that last word.

It was, he thought, a useful way of keeping himself on the ball, keeping himself going. Of surviving. Of fending off petty routine, reminiscences, nostalgia.

His conversion – as unexpected as it was distressing – was about to happen, that very evening, in an underground train.

To get to the porte de Clignancourt, Wallace had to go right across Paris. There he was, slap in the middle of April, riding along on the métro. He'd made this same journey nearly half a century previously, just after the war, when he'd come to study at the Sorbonne for a year.

Like that last time, he started counting the stations still to go before he had to get off.

Suddenly, he didn't know why or how it happened, he was taken aback by the significance of the words 'here and now' of which he was so fond.

And at that very moment, the words vanished into thin air!

Wallace concentrated hard, dug deep within himself to recapture the rhythm, the steady beat of these words which had disintegrated into a thousand fragments.

But 'here and now' had, suddenly, evaporated. There was no way he could get a hold on them, not even by stealth.

He'd been abandoned. He'd been given the slip. This 'expression' had lost its texture. Its consistency had gone; its grain had gone. Wallace concentrated hard, made repeated efforts to catch it unawares, to grasp it – all to no avail as it slithered away, slippery as an eel.

Had 'here and now' ever existed?

That same feeling of bewilderment which overcame him when he tried to visualise the cosmos, when he let his mind play on the planets and the solar system, on the infinite mystery of life, closed in on Wallace and made his head spin.

It was rush hour. The crowds were streaming into the métro. All the folding seats were up, making room for the flood of passengers to swamp the carriage. For a moment Wallace wondered whether they were all real; then he wondered if he was.

But, against his back, against his shoulders, he felt the warmth from other people's backs, from other people's shoulders, he became aware of his breath mingling together with other people's, coming into contact with the solid mass of human beings and inanimate objects;

bit by bit he pulled himself together.

With his left hand he clung tightly to one of the door handles so he could feel the warmth given off by the metal. With the other he fingered the velvety silk of his salmon-pink shirt which he had treated himself to for the trip. He found it still gave him the same pleasure: 'I'm here, I really am here,' he said to himself.

Despite this reassurance, here and now had, quite obviously, disappeared! Spirited away, miraculously, like a dove in a magician's top hat, went Time.

Confronted with this emptiness, this inertia, this void, this illusion which he relied on to bolster his days, Wallace wanted to make a thorough investigation, in the few minutes he had left – the train had just left the station at Les Halles – of this new situation.

No sooner had he called the words 'here and now' to mind than, in one spectacular leap, they converged upon the past; clinging to it, relentlessly expanding and rein-forcing it.

But then, conversely, they became one and the same as the future.

There was no way round it. Despite the risk of skidding hither and thither on a moving pavement of indeterminate speed and destination, he had to opt for the one or the other.

At first it was imperative – the train was pulling into the gare du Nord – to hold fast to the idea that 'here and now' was no more than an empty shell, a bubble. Not even an empty shell, not even a bubble: they at least had outlines!

What had to be done, crucially, was to accept the notion that 'here and now' was as nothing. Absolutely nothing. But then, he had to chose sides: would it be 'the past' or 'the future'?

It would have been disturbing, that much was certain, were he not able to get back on course.

The past – apart from History with a capital H – his own past did nothing to inspire him.

Although Wallace had achieved a considerable number of targets during his long life, his past gave him the impression of being cramped, petty and absurdly sub-jective.

What was more, any account of it by other people, any shared memories were so tarnished by error, so fettered by personal feelings that he could barely recognise himself in their sometimes murky, sometimes flatteringly hazy recollections.

In his mind's eye, 'once upon a time' was a butterfly net, an elephant trap. Until now he had chosen to skirt round it and keep going straight ahead. 'I'm all for living in the here and now!' he would say over and over again. But if here and now didn't exist, had never existed, wasn't he going to have to opt for the future?

His own future, there was no use denying it, was

visibly shrinking, visibly dwindling.

That was as far as Wallace had got when the train stopped at the end of the line.

He got out of the carriage and made his way up flight after flight of stairs. On the way, he thought to himself that he must have missed the escalator: but was there one at the porte de Clignancourt?

As he was leaving the station, a long-haired young man in a leather blouson held the door open for him. He dashed through with a hasty word of thanks; he was sorry it meant leaving behind him that distinctive smell of the Paris métro. It was that bitter-sweet smell that used to waft into his memory, back there, in his wood-land home.

Outside, he bought a newspaper at the newsstand and waited for Pauline. He invariably arrived too early for things.

For a few seconds he wavered between wanting to see her again and wanting to dive back into the métro station so he could avoid his friend's face as it must look these days; the face that, by a cruel twist of fate, could not fail to mask the one she had had when she was twenty.

But as he had come so far for this reunion, he decided to wait and take what was coming.

On the other side of the street, there was Pauline,

already calling out to him in her best English: 'Hey, Wallace, Wally, it's me.'

She was making the first move. She was frightened that he wouldn't pick her out from beneath the insidious ruins of the passing years. What a relief, for him, to have been so readily recognised.

'Pauline, *Linou*!'

He crossed over to where she stood.

'You're still as handsome as ever,' she said, giving him a peck on the cheek.

He took both her hands, raised them to his lips and placed a gentle kiss, just like he used to, on each wrist. And on one arm was the bracelet he had once given her.

'I still wear it.'

'The past,' he sighed.

'But we're here and now.'

He was tempted to tell her about his recent experience; but she was so excited at seeing him again that he didn't want to spoil it by talking at her.

He bent down, gently took off her tortoise-shell spectacles and gazed into her eyes.

'Still the same blue,' he said with satisfaction.

She smiled. He smiled back.

Between them, something indefinable was happening. Something that arched across the years. A quiver through the body, a surge of vitality they thought had subsided.

It made them touching despite their wrinkles; beguiling despite their thickening waistlines.

Hand in hand they walked towards their old bistro.

The decor had changed; so had the owners. The tables, with their marble tops and ornate legs, had not.

They sat down opposite each other.

'Like before,' he murmured.

'Like now,' she said.

Yet again he wanted to tell her what he had just been through; to lay bare the truth or the falseness of the words, of the state of mind which she in turn seemed unable to handle correctly.

Once again he held back, asking: 'What have all these years been like?'

'Difficult. I'll tell you one of these days. What about you?'

'It's been a long time . . .'

'You haven't changed,' she said. 'You've only ever liked here and now. Just think back . . .'

He thought he could catch a note of reproach in her voice: what was it in their past she was trying to hint at?

'Are we going to have lunch?' he said suddenly, avoiding her question.

'Fine. I'm free. What about you?'

'Yes, me too.'

'How many days are you staying?'

'As many as I want.'

*

They shared the bread, the wine, the laughter.

By the end of the meal everything was suffused by a cheerful silence. Other customers, their surroundings, everything melted away into the background.

The marble table had been cleared. They leant their elbows on its bare surface and gazed deeply, steadily into each other's eyes.

So steadily, so unwaveringly that the seasons combined, merged the one with another.

So steadily, so intensely that here and now suddenly became forever.

The Boy Beneath the Streetlamp

Tony was bored with dragging round the temple at Karnak, packed in with that gaggle of tourists.

His sandals were full of sand and gravel and they were hurting his feet. His mother had insisted on him putting on his khaki socks and a pair of shorts that came down to his knees. What was worse was the wide-brimmed straw hat which was supposed to stop him getting sunburn; they were the only ones in the whole family who had the delicate, overly white complexion inherited from a distant Caucasian ancestor. Tony felt like a freak in that get-up, topped off by that ridiculous headgear. What was more, Noda would insist on treating her son like a little kid, grabbing hold of his hand and dragging him along behind her: 'Leave me alone, Mum. I'm fifteen. I'm not a baby any more.'

His mother turned toward him. Her smooth, pretty face was surrounded by a mass of curly auburn hair above which hovered the same sort of hat as her son's. Hers was held in place by a bright red ribbon, dotted with tiny flowers, which wound round the crown and came down to form a knot under her chin.

'Quick, darling, quick. We're going to lose the group!'

That's just what Tony wanted: to lose the group, to get out of this dreary procession, not to have to put up with the guide's droning voice! The man's long, spindly head bobbed up and down every now and again above the sea of other heads. Hopping from English into German, then into French, he struggled to bring alive the grandeur of the place and the splendour of its vanished past. His feats of memory and his eloquence were all pointless.

'This is your country, Tony. When all's said and done, you'll have to get to know something about its history.'

From time to time packs of ragged children circled the tourists. Chattering and nodding, holding their open hands out in front of them, they begged for money as if it were a joke but with a persistence that nothing could shake.

In the end the guide, having run out of invectives, reached breaking point and landed a kick in amongst the gang of children. He was soon joined by the holiday-makers who waved their fly-switches in the air before bringing them down hard, with a dull thud, on the grubby, darting, tunic-clad children.

Even Noda had joined in. Horrified, Tony had grabbed the fly-switch out of his mother's hands and stamped on it.

'How could you, Mum?'

A lad of about twelve wearing a sky-blue cotton skullcap broke away from the group. He bent down, picked up the broken object and held it out to its owner, saying softly: '*Maalesh, maalesh.*' (Never mind, it's not important.)

He had a mocking yet kindly smile which mortified Tony all the more.

Noda, who for years had thought of nothing but dresses, cocktails and the interior design of her fine home, had suddenly been bitten by the 'culture' bug. It was all the rage at the time! Whether she was in Egypt, France, Greece or Italy, she would now go from museum to museum, from monument to monument, taking photographs right, left and centre. When she got back she would treat groups of family and friends to interminable slide shows.

'Here, if you want, I'll lend you my camera,' she suggested, to placate her son a little.

He refused point-blank. He was sickened by the mere idea of adding yet more nondescript views to the pile that already existed, of trivialising sunsets and faces hewn in stone, of squashing timeless monuments onto flat paper.

In the distance he could hear the enthusiastic squawks from the crowd and could make out the short and frequent flashes from their cameras – and all the while the colossal statues kept their eyes fixed on the horizon, locked away in the silence of another world.

The ruins covered a wide area. Tony had just noticed an obelisk which reminded him of the one in the middle of the place de la Concorde. His mother seized her opportunity: 'Well done, Tony!' she said encouragingly as she took a look at her *Michelin Blue Guide*. 'The obelisk in Paris was given to France in 1831 by Mohammed Ali. The other one, the one you've just seen over there, behind that line of columns, is Queen Hatshepsut's.'

Tony sniggered.

'What are you laughing at?'

'You should have heard yourself saying that funny name, Mum!'

Noda was sorry she had brought her son with her for the Easter holidays; he spoiled all her enjoyment. She tried again a couple times to tell the story; she'd done her homework before the trip, she'd done it for herself but above all for him. She acted out the legend of Amun, the god of gods; she breathed life into that unrivalled victor, Rameses II. But Tony took no interest and went on with his daydream.

Remembering that her son was particularly good at maths, she tried to rouse his interest by reeling off some numbers and measurements: 'Did you know that a seated colossus is more than fifteen metres high? That the pylons . . .'

'What's a pylon?'

'They're those huge towers on either side of the stone doorway. Well, each one is a hundred and thirteen metres wide, forty-three metres high and fifteen metres thick. Just imagine, Tony, fifteen metres thick!'

Exhilarated by her newfound knowledge, she went on: 'And then there's the Hypostyle Hall . . .'

'Hypostyle, what's that?'

'All these words come from ancient Greek.'

'Ancient Greek!' he scoffed. 'Since when have you known anything about ancient Greek, Mum?'

Her son's behaviour was verging on the insolent. Noda had to stop herself snapping a reprimand at him. For some time now she had been feeling guilty about her preference for this eldest son of hers; admittedly, until then he had been a good pupil in his Catholic boarding school and had not been any trouble at home. When he reached puberty the fatherless child – Noda had been widowed after only five years of marriage – had started showing signs of a rebelliousness that only a father's influence could have curbed. She gazed at him indulgently; it was neither the time nor the place to have a row – or to play the card of filial obedience. She decided to hold her tongue; all the more so because they were getting near a packed crowd of tourists gathered round the guide. Standing on a stool which he lugged around with him everywhere, the guide was churning out his patter in a monotonous, grating voice.

'The Hypostyle Hall,' she went on more quietly, ignoring the impertinent remark, 'is a room where the ceiling is held up on columns. We'll be going in there in a minute.'

And she immediately started regurgitating numbers again: 'This room is a hundred metres wide by fifty-two metres long. The ceiling is supported on thirty-two columns arranged in sixteen rows . . .'

In an attempt to get her son interested, Noda became dramatic and tremulous in turns as if she was reciting the most beautiful of all poems. She even managed to make him relent. Tony thought she was overdoing it but that she looked touching in her tight cotton dress which sported huge yellow flowers and fitted rather too snugly over her bust and hips. Her necklines, too low as always, gave a glimpse of the swell of her breasts. Tottering on high heels – her vanity forbade her to wear sandals – she walked heron-like on slender legs that were out of all proportion and seemed constantly on the verge of breaking.

Tony offered her his arm and smiled at her. In a burst of gratitude, she kissed him. He was now so tall that his mother's kiss landed on his earlobe, smearing him with lipstick. She managed to remove the scarlet marks with her delicate cotton handkerchief, and, with a nervous little smile, apologised as she did so.

He found his mother irritating and yet touching at the same time. He occasionally wondered what he was doing, being there with her. Wouldn't they both have been better off putting between them a certain distance which could have reinforced their affection for one another?

Tony would have preferred to go over the ruins alone: to climb to the top of one of the pylons as the fancy took him so that he could gaze down, in one sweeping glance, over this realm of death and the afterlife; to sit between the knees of a god or a goddess; to straddle one of the forty rams ranged either side of an avenue; even to cool himself off in the waters of the sacred pool.

Dusk was darkening the sky and beginning to cast its iridescence over the ruins. Had he been surrounded by silence, Tony would have enjoyed seeing twilight fall on these magnificent enigmas. But Noda had puckered up her lips and, misty eyed, was weaving ridiculously affectionate pet names round him: 'My treasure, my little chick, light of my life, heart of my heart.'

The guided visit was nearly over. The blue of the sky disappeared behind a deep layer of ebony blackness, soon to be inlaid with a garland of stars.

Just as Noda was getting into one of the many horse-drawn carriages which were to take the tourists back to their hotels, Tony announced: 'I'm walking back. Don't worry, I'll be back for dinner.'

It was too late to call him back. With one last wave of his hand, Tony disappeared down an alleyway and was already dashing off toward the nearest small town. Noda consoled herself by musing that sometimes the best thing to do was to allow her son free rein, especially if it was for something so unimportant.

When she saw his back from a distance, Noda was amazed by her son's speed, by his bearing . . . They were already those of a full-grown man.

*

Tony had no idea what to expect.

He took off his straw hat, crushing the crown as he slipped it under his arm, and tipped the sand out of his shoes. Then, abandoning the soft ground to get on to a tarmac path, he set off again. Allowed to be himself at last, he was carefree, foot-loose and happy!

In the distance he could see the main road to Cairo, but went off in the opposite direction, towards the bridge which crossed the canal and led to the village of Luxor. To get through the village he would use some of the alleys he had spotted on one of the maps in the *Blue Guide* and had jotted down in his notebook. That's the route he would take, in his own time, to get back to the Palace Hotel where his mother would be waiting for him before dinner.

Having won his freedom, he suddenly wanted to take a new look at some of the colossal figures and those human-headed sphinxes which the tourists had as good as obliterated, eradicated with their waving arms and their chattering. Tony walked away from the little town and, humming to himself, turned off toward the temple which stood not far from the Nile.

All alone on this deserted stretch of road, lit by the occasional street lamp, he followed the high outer wall swathed in darkness. At the end of the narrow path the fifth – and last – streetlight shielded a watery flame beneath its dust-stained cover. Its bright, yellowy glow, only a little less feeble than the others, tinged the patch of ground round its blackened foot with a circle of light that seemed to have been drawn with a pair of compasses.

With his back to it, a boy was squatting against the cast-iron lamppost.

As he got nearer to him, Tony recognised the boy's sky-blue skullcap: it was the young lad who had picked up the fly-switch and given it back to Noda.

Not a sound, not a footfall would make him move a muscle. Tony stopped and waited, trying to understand why he was so still.

At last he caught sight of an open book, lying between the young boy's legs on the folds of a baggy striped tunic.

The child was trailing his forefinger, line by line, down the page bathed in its faint pool of light, and was slowly struggling to spell out the words. It was as if he were sampling an exquisite titbit, savouring it and chewing it, then finally swallowing it, letting its goodness mingle with his flesh and blood to bring them back to life.

From time to time the bowed back straightened, as if the reader were trying to save his eyes, to rest them. In those moments, the boy would look up at the temple and gaze at it, still mouthing the newly acquired syllables or phrases so that he could commit them to memory more actively.

His whole being gave off an air of contemplation, of resilience.

Keeping his distance, Tony stared without moving. Suddenly he started to hear the beating of his own heart. Suddenly these stones, this boy's quest, welling up from the depths of time, became one with the present. Suddenly the whole of History, all the legends, were embodied in the puny body of an adolescent puzzling out a few symbols.

Every evening Saïd escaped from the yelling, the bleating, the whimpering and the shouts which filled his overcrowded hovel. Packed into the one room, lit by the one oil lamp, his father, mother, grandparents, nine brothers and sisters, a donkey and a goat, all lived together.

Every evening, sitting as scribes have done throughout the ages, Saïd took his place in the centre of the hazy ring of light, and became engrossed in his reading: he was carefree, foot-loose and happy! He was himself, at last.

Driven by a strange thirst which each day's cavorting and the few charitable coins couldn't slake, the child was trying to understand, to learn – without knowing where it would all lead him.

After a moment, Tony set off again toward the lamp-post. Treading softly he reached the narrow carpet of light and stood still once more.

The other boy recognised him immediately and gestured to him to sit down beside him.

By throwing it as far as he could, Tony got rid of the huge straw hat which had given him the vacuous, demure look of the well-bred child! As he squatted down he was embarrassed because his shorts were tight and showed his thighs and knees.

Taking no notice, Saïd put his arm round his shoulders. 'I've got some words I don't understand. Can you help me?'

Tony agreed gratefully.

As they went on with the reading, they stopped, now on one word, now on another. Then, when they started to read again, they played with changing the pitch or giving a rhythm to the sentences, thus giving each syllable its own inflexion and musical quality.

An amicable, fun-filled hour slipped by.

Suddenly, remembering his mother, Tony thought how worried she would be; her feverish anxiety would mean that she would unleash the police in the hunt for her son. He explained to Saïd why he had to go, that very minute. As Tony got up, he rummaged around in his pockets, scraped together a few small coins and held them out to him: 'You're not a tourist, you're my brother! Keep them!' the boy said cheerfully without seeming to take offence. 'What's your name?'

'Tony. What's yours?'

'Saïd.'

In his turn he pulled an old penknife out of his pocket and asked Tony to scratch his name into the cast-iron foot of the lamppost.

'That way you'll be here every evening.'

'I'll come back.'

'I'll be right here. I'm always here. Always. Until I go to university . . .'

He waited to see what effect his words would have.

'You'll see, it'll happen.'

'I believe you. It's got to happen.'

Saïd tore a piece of squared paper out of his mauve exercise book and held it out to Tony: 'Keep this. If, later on, you change . . . if we change, this piece of paper will help us recognise each other, anywhere!'

As he was leaving, Tony remembered the broad-brimmed hat and walked over to get it. Picking it up, he tried to hide it behind his back. Suddenly Saïd suggested a surprising swap: 'You take my cap and give me your hat!'

The boy seemed delighted by his own suggestion. He could see himself wearing the standard item of tourist's headcover; he could imagine the amazed curiosity he would get from his family and the gang of urchins who were his begging companions.

Tony did not wait to be asked twice. He put the straw hat on his new friend's shaved head – and it came down right to his ears. Settling the sky-blue skullcap on his curly mass of hair he set off, walking on air, toward the Palace Hotel.

Before going into the lobby Tony carefully rolled the little cotton cap into a ball and stuffed it into his pocket. He had no intention of saying anything to Noda about his encounter.

As soon as his mother spotted him, she threw herself on him. Hugging him and smothering him with kisses she breathlessly bombarded him with questions. 'Where were you? I was out of my mind. Ten more minutes and I was going to call the police.'

The forceful tone of voice he used to answer was new to her: 'I was paying a visit to the gods!'

'The gods?'

'I even met a scribe.'

'A scribe? In Karnak, in Luxor? You're wrong, Tony; you saw the Seated Scribe, the one with glass eyes, in the museum in Cairo. Don't you remember, we went together?'

'Don't go on, Mum; I'm telling you, I saw a scribe.'

'All right, all right, as you wish,' she said, not wanting to stir up an argument.

Sometimes her son deliberately made her angry. He had most likely got lost in the ruins and been scared. Now he was saying the first thing that came into his head, so as not to look foolish.

'Look!' said Tony, cut to the quick and trying to prove that he was not dreaming. 'Look!'

He held out the scrap of paper that Saïd had torn from his mauve exercise book.

'What's that . . . ? Grammar!'

'Precisely . . . it's grammar.'

'But that's the one thing you really hate!'

'Not now.'

'Not now? What do you mean? You could at least tell

me what you're talking about.'

Tony was just about to speak when he was checked by his mother's appearance. He thought she looked too made-up, too flashy. What would she make of what he said? How would she interpret or even pervert what he had felt?

Noda, throwing simpering glances at the neighbouring tables as she powdered her nose, smiled into her pocket mirror. She repeated her question without thinking: 'I'm listening, Tony. I'm right, aren't I? You hated grammar, didn't you?'

'Not now,' he repeated, determined not to say anything.

She tried one last time to get him to give in. She stroked his hand, promised him a moped for his birthday. But his lips were sealed.

Seeing the dessert trolley at the far end of the dining room, Noda snapped her fingers at the headwaiter and called him over in her shrill voice. This behaviour infuriated Tony; he shuddered, feeling his cheeks turn bright red, then scowled.

She knew he loved his food so, still trying to draw him out, she said to the waiter as she stared indulgently at her silent, pigheaded son: 'Would you please give the gentleman a double serving of chocolate mousse.'

Sliding his hand deep into his pocket, Tony held the blue skullcap tight in his hand and fingered it. Slowly his smile returned.

Time and the Body

'As for the march of time,
consider it as nothing
in the midst of a permanent forever.'
Rainer Maria Rilke

'I don't understand,' she mumbled, 'how I gave birth
. . . how on earth did I give birth to this old man!'

An old man, that's what her son was now! Looking
the facts in the face or even being offended by them got
her nowhere: what she saw did not fit in with the way she
was or the way she felt. Her own son, an old man of
sixty-six? There were times when she could ignore the
evidence by living life to the full, by seizing each passing
moment, by pretending to forget the truth . . . and
forgetting it.

But at other times a gesture, a word would stop her in
her tracks. Her flight of fancy would come to an abrupt
end and she would suddenly find herself confronted with
the pot belly, the scrawny neck, the liver marks on the
back of the hands, the stooping back, the lumbering walk.

Her refusal to accept the passing of time was wearing
her out; as were her efforts to turn a blind eye to the way

he looked these days. To her mind it was a parody of that earlier look – remote and youthful – he had had when he was nine or twenty or, at a pinch, even thirty.

How come, given all that abundant affection of hers, she had failed to keep the years at bay, to protect her child? Why, as the years had come and gone, had she not been able to prevent his fine face from withering? How come she had not managed to thin out the little shower of wrinkles – as and when they had appeared – or put right the bones and muscles as they collapsed deep inside him? She had been so caring, how come she had not, at least at times, melted those layers of ice in his soul?

She often blamed herself for not having been able to hold back time for him, as she had managed to do for herself, despite the twenty years she had on him.

At night she would sometimes dream of a muddy pit into which her son was sinking. At the edge of the hole, with her legs braced and her two hands under his arms, she would be pulling his heavy frame from the mud and grunting like a bargee.

She would surface from these nightmares, bathed in sweat, her head pounding. No, she would never be able to bear seeing him slide into old age, even if it was to be with her and to take up his place, beside her, in the ranks of the elderly.

*

For her younger daughters, the transition had been trouble free. As she pored over the most recent photographs of them, she was quite unmoved and found it quite natural to imagine them being old. All three of them lived far away, continents apart; their absence had not upset her, nor had the fact that she saw them less and less often. Between herself and her daughters a relaxed, trusting, sisterly affection had very quickly grown up; the umbilical cord, having never been very substantial, had faded away, leaving no trace.

When life all around her was drab, when her horizons closed in upon her and the days offered little to stimulate her, she would stare ever harder at her son, trying to spot the signs of fatigue, migraine, rheumatism, the sound of a groan. The slightest change in him would send ripples through her own body like an echo laden with warning.

Her unruly heart would always go on being a cradle, a grotto, a shelter for him. She would have liked to let this elderly child of hers climb onto her shoulders, as she used to do in times gone by, so she could whisk him away, far from any troubles.

No matter where she was, she would run to him if he needed help. Standing firm against real or imagined threats, she became the she-wolf to protect him from the wolves, she kept herself at the ready to ward off difficulties, to hack down discontent, to drive away all the sluggishness of old age which made such a cruel mockery of his existence.

At other times – if the sun broke through the mists or if something new happened – she would march away, carrying the anxiety off with her, blotting it out in the exhilaration of the moment and in the passion of her stride.

From time to time she felt jealous of those who had died young. Friends or relations who had been lost along the way, and in ever growing numbers, she realised.

In effect, she begrudged the fact that they had taken with them that freshness, that youthful complexion and that sparkle which had escaped the wear and tear of life and were of no further use to them. It was absurd, but sometimes she even dreamt of robbing them of all this unspoiled youth, all this spare vitality, so she could breathe it into her son.

Then she would see him as a boy again, resplendent as he swam to victory in blue-glazed swimming pools; the handsome young man who, whisking her off the ground to break the news that he had passed his exams, would whirl her round and round; or she would see – there were those shining black eyes of his and the dark hair that went with them – that fine young thirty year old who had no thoughts of settling down.

She had lost her own father when he was thirty; her husband had died at twenty-seven; her mother had lived only into her thirty-third year . . . But, not being able to bear the depression of inactivity for long, she recovered from those bereavements, those agonising wrenches with a renewed taste for living.

Having come close to the depths of the abyss she sought safety by hurling herself at life in one swift lunge of her whole being. She burst out of grief, out of misery, with an unbridled appetite for sparkling light and activity, dashing off here, there and everywhere, listening, watching, keeping in touch with what was new in the world. Even Time got breathless trying to keep up with her.

She compared her existence to that of a tree with countless branches; she fretted over the thought that one day the sap, no longer surging up from its roots, might drain from those very branches.

At other times, when it occurred to her that she and her son had had all they could have wanted – since here they were, alive and well – she was profoundly thankful to nature as a whole: she would touch wood and kiss the ground even though she only half believed in these superstitions.

When she thought about it, she did not envy the dead; they were safe from change but robbed of breath; smooth-skinned and beautiful for eternity, but deprived of passion and pleasure. All those who had died young were missing out on delights great and small; what did they now know of a word babbled by a child, a greeting, a film, a treat, summer rain, a meeting, a bud, a ray of sunshine or of moonlight . . .

*

In another of her nightmares, she pictured herself marching at the head of a battalion of old men and women. They followed her with faltering steps but their whimpering voices were slowing her down.

At other times, perched at the top of a family tree, she gazed at the tribe climbing up: a broken, withered, crippled hoard, all born of her.

Being one for hot-headed spirits and plump, firm bodies with their sweetly acid smell, she was sickened at the thought that she was the source of a pale and exhausted bloodline whose fond eyes turned up towards her, their begetter. Their sallow faces and their disappointed dreams merely irritated and saddened her.

Yet she always set herself free from these bleak, introspective visions by projecting herself into another time. Into a single moment; a distillation of all other times. This ability, this instinct of hers plunged her into a fluid, flowing substance, as huge as a galaxy, which smoothed out the wrinkles in what she saw.

Deep in his chair her son was sleeping.

She stared at his stomach spilling over onto his thighs, his splayed knees, his feet lounging in patent-leather slippers. The spent pipe lay on the carpet next to a bowl of fruit, a dirty cup and some scattered newspapers.

The sight of this shambles brought a flush of anger to her cheeks. It was at times like this that she was sorry he had never married; a wife, she thought, would have dealt with this mess.

Glossing over the intermediate link of grandsons who would, no doubt, be getting on for forty by now, she was also sorry that she did not have any great-grand-children. She could imagine them, here, now, bursting with health and laughter, arguing loudly, giving her a kiss and dashing off.

Then, from her balcony she could have looked down at them in admiration as they roared off on large, brightly coloured motorbikes.

Later, she remembered the time when her son was twelve and that first evening when she had wanted to go out to meet a man friend. The child had laid down on the floor, blocking the doorway: 'You're not going out!'

His face was ashen, the thought of it still made her shiver. She had hesitated. She had gone over to the telephone, on the verge of cancelling her date. Then she went back to him: 'I have to go out.'

For both of them – for him, for her – it was imperative not to give in. She tried to lift him up, pull him to her, talk to him, explain. He stayed put, stiffening his muscles and flattening himself against the floorboards.

'You're not going out!'

His tone annoyed her; she took orders from no one.

'I am going out!'

Before going off, she called to her daughters for help.

'It's all right, Mum. You go!'

Her heart wavered as she stepped over her son. Her younger girls surrounded their brother, jeering and laughing, pushing her out – to live, to be happy.

'Go on. Quick.'

As she walked away she could still hear the child bawling behind the door, but she carried on walking.

In the evening, he was waiting for her. She lay down beside him on the bed.

'I have a right to live my life,' she murmured gently. 'I have a right.'

Later he had had a life of his own. She had never interfered.

She smiled as she remembered the scene, and other scenes too . . .

'In those days, I was beautiful. I can say that now: I was beautiful!'

She remembered the fact without bitterness, as if inside her decaying body, the other body was still wide awake.

Her own infirmities had always seemed easier to bear than those of her family. Her whole body was gradually deteriorating, but without dimming her gaze, without crushing her hopes. As for her face, she made no attempt to hide the signs of the passage of time, but remedied only what was within her power to deal with; the movement in her joints, the straightness of her back and the state of her hair.

Forgetting the mess and her irritation, she went over to her son and was touched as she looked at the heavy, crumpled body.

Putting her small hand on his stubby, motionless one

she stroked it several times.

At length she bent over and placed a lingering kiss on the forehead of the man as he slept.

Feeling the touch of his mother's lips, he slowly stirred.

A faint smile of gratitude floated up from the drowsiness only to sink back down into it.

'Mother,' he muttered weakly. 'Mother.'

She straightened up.

Very lightly, she placed her open hand on the greying head.

Waves of tenderness flooded through her body.

Eggs and Improvisation

The alarm clock stuffed under my plump pillow started jangling at six in the morning, reminding me that it was time for my music. I practised every day, before the school bus came to pick me up at about seven thirty.

Already the sun was shining through the closed shutters. It was still summer and the heat pricked at my skin; there was sweat on my neck and under my arms. The lofty mosquito net surrounding my bed made an airy, almost magical cage.

Cairo, with its town centre and its suburbs, sparkled in the distance. Our villa, like many others – several of which teetered on the edge of the Nile – stood some way off, surrounded by a high-walled garden. It was 1932.

First with my elbows, then with every inch of my body, I pressed down on the pillow to stifle the ringing that could well have woken my young brother, asleep in the bed opposite.

I got up and, just briefly, went and gazed at him as he slept. I adore gazing at people's faces, and this was the only time I could study his features in peace. The rest of the time he was a fidget, constantly on the move as if he was being run by a dynamo.

Leaning over him in his quieter moments, I could see,

just for a fraction of a second, the face of a cherub, veiled and softened by the fine mesh of the mosquito net.

He was seven. We were born three years apart; at that age, it makes a big difference. Unusually for this country, my brother had curls and fair hair; a deep cleft in his chin made him look both sulky and naïve. Just at that moment I couldn't see his lively blue eyes. I smiled at the sight of his very round, very soft cheeks which were as likely to deserve a kiss as a pinch or a smack.

I never missed the chance of giving him a good slap during our countless brawls. Half stingray, half jellyfish, he would cling to me as we clashed. With my hair in a mess and my calves, my arms and my hands all sporting the traces of his little teeth, it was only by making the most enormous effort that I could extricate myself from these spats.

My brother used to fly into massive rages. That was when he would kick over the traces and launch an attack on me, his very own sister. Beneath my skinny frame and my outward patience I had hidden in me phenomenal levels of resistance and aggression. And I was a head taller than him. These storms were brief and never did any harm to our enduring friendship.

Our fights were always playful and sportsman-like and there was never a spiteful word. No doubt they allowed my brother to let off steam; they taught me, later on, despite being placid and shy, to face up to life's hard knocks.

Our English governess exercised, without the slightest misgiving, corporal punishment as practised in the best British public schools. If ever I thought my brother was under threat of a whack from Miss Boone's ruler I would stand in front of her so she couldn't get past. Puny though I was, I could manage to make her back down. The sight of this pale little lass standing rigid, eyes smouldering, intimidated Miss Boone. She would hide the ruler behind her back, and make us both go without dessert for three days.

Our complicity had nothing to do with intimate chats or shared secrets. My young brother's hot-blooded temperament was, in every respect, a complete contrast to my diffident nature which, none the less, concealed a violent inner turmoil. I don't know what it was that created this bond between us; more than anything it was merely because there were just the two of us, kept at arm's length by our parents and off-loaded, as a pair, onto Miss Boone and her principles.

As far as principles were concerned, she had some positive ones which were character building and others which were questionable and pernickety. We admired her sporting prowess, her tennis skills, her long-distance swimming and her delight in dancing. We loathed the shrill, refined voice which she used on the telephone, the haughty way she treated the servants, her cold fury and her patronising attitude to everything that was not British. We loved her and hated her in turn.

*

Our white villa was one of those 'Italianate' houses built towards the end of the nineteenth century. They were all embellished with colonnades, wide front steps and balconies. You can see them, even nowadays, virtually anywhere right round the Mediterranean.

Inside, what gave our house its character, and what remains firmly fixed in my memory, was the immense open space that rose between the ground floor and the first floor. This empty, circular area, surrounded by a wrought iron and brass balustrade, linked the huge downstairs entrance hall to a curved balcony upstairs, behind which were the bedrooms.

On evenings when there were guests, Miss Boone, in a long dress, would be discreetly making sure that everything was going to plan, so we, my little brother and I, would take advantage of her absence and kneel down at the foot of the balustrade and, through the gaps in the bars, gaze at the scene below us.

First, the guests arrived; women in sumptuous, shimmering gowns, men in tails. But even more importantly, there was our mother, far more beautiful than any of the other women; I can still see her in that cloud of pink chiffon, the flared skirt, the close-fitting bodice and the long stole floating round her bare shoulders. After a while we would start looking out for our father; despite his height and handsome figure, he eluded our searching eyes, for he always kept in the background, almost like an outsider at the party.

'But where's Daddy?' my young brother would ask.

It became a game to be the first to spot him.

Then the banquet was paraded in: there were all sorts of main courses and side dishes, piled on huge silver salvers and held aloft by a dozen servants (the word already made me wince) in long colourful tunics. These servants marched, in procession, toward the dining room and we had all the time we wanted to admire, from high in our eyrie, the mouth-watering feast.

At dawn the whole house continued to sleep as my brother and I, hearts racing, went barefoot down the grand staircase, treading underfoot the Chinese pattern on the red carpet.

We would pile the tastiest leftovers from the lavish spread onto enormous plates and then crouch down together under the great long table, hidden from view beneath the floor-length tablecloth.

Mixing sweet with savoury, meat with fish, desserts with hors d'œuvres, we feasted, in secret and mutual delight, on the exquisite food we had been ogling all that time the night before.

But to get back to the music practice. Having woken up each morning at six o'clock and thrown a flowery dressing gown over my pyjamas, I would go down that same staircase – this time with little enthusiasm – to the music room. There, on a magnificent, shiny black Pleyel grand which I was about to abuse with my incompetence, I struggled for thirty minutes – thumping up and down the scales and a few other basic exercises jotted down in a blue manuscript book.

Miss Boone used to leave her door onto the circular balcony open a crack. She said I should do the same downstairs so that as she lay in her bed the sounds I made – she had particularly acute hearing – would flow freely up to her, whilst my parents' slumber, protected by firmly closed double doors, would remain disturbed.

Any lengthy silence would have her leaping out of bed. Leaning over the balustrade, she would scold: 'I'm listening, and I can't hear anything!'

At other times, after running a quick comb through her hair, she would pull a dress on over her nightgown and hurtle down the stairs which separated us. Suddenly I would see her appear in the doorway to the music room. Pulling herself up to her full, diminutive height and with her nose as pink as her cheeks, she would screw up her tiny blue eyes and say sharply: 'You're not going to get any better like that!'

She always managed to keep such a pleasant look on her healthy, glowing face that, in spite of everything, I was often tempted to confess to her my complete absence of any aptitude for that kind of music. But, as this sort of training, like good manners, was part and parcel of that proper education which she had been entrusted to administer, she would have been unable either to understand or condone.

I was much more inclined to improvise. I had had a go several times, fiddling about on the keyboard, but I hadn't got anywhere. I had no talent for that either.

So I dreamed of other rhythms, other sounds, other conventions, other expressions, other colours . . . which would help me to breathe, to blossom!

At school my daily encounter with the piano teacher, Mademoiselle Petitpas, bored me rigid. She was an elderly maiden lady with a pasty face, yellowing hair and, behind the thick lenses of her silver-rimmed glasses, you could see she had a squint. I pictured her in an endless purgatory, tied to her piano stool and running her gnarled hands with their nicotine-stained nails over the black and white keys, condemned to do nothing but coax eternal scales out of them.

But for the time being, it was me glued to the piano stool, hammering out monotonous noises and feeding them into Miss Boone's vigilant ear.

What was about to follow was considerably more entertaining.

This was the moment when Soliman, our Sudanese under-chef, would appear. The usual time for 'breakfast', as we called it in English, was seven o'clock and I would eat with my brother and the governess. Well before that, Soliman would glide towards me in his long white robes bearing a glass of ice-cold blackberry cordial and a plateful of sweet pastries on a large tray.

As he found his chores harder to accept than did anyone else, he seemed to take an interest in mine and used to try to alleviate my drudgery. Soliman would put the precious tray down on a chair, conveniently placed to my right, then stand back against one of the walls, facing me. As soon as I raised a hand to lift the glass to take a sip or pick at the biscuits or the little cakes – the other hand would still be going on automatically with its exercises – an expression of delight and satisfaction would spread across his face.

I found the minutes flew by as he stared at me with his smiling young eyes and I admired the curves of his ebony features which bore on each cheek the brand of four tribal marks. Often I would see him edge nearer so he could look at the way my hands moved over the keyboard. The way my fingers moved to make the sounds stream out seemed to fascinate him. I noticed, too, that he winced with pain each time I played a wrong note.

Morning after morning, Soliman could not resist indulging in the pleasure of indulging me more and more.

Soon he was bringing croissants, doughnuts, brioches, date jam, orange marmalade or large glasses of flavoured milk. Then one day he excelled himself. First the exquisite aroma of toast and fried bacon wafted in and then I saw Soliman himself come through the door, walk toward me and present me with a large plate on which were sizzling three fried eggs. Their white edges, crisp and golden, were still quivering; the yellows, a perfect circle, were bulging to bursting point.

But how, without stopping the music, was I going to do justice to this phenomenon?

I was on the horns of a cruel dilemma. As I carried on with my exercises, I turned to Soliman and shot him an enquiring look.

Both of us reached the same conclusion at exactly the same moment. Soliman would take my place and I would take his – and the tray. I felt instinctively that the young Sudanese man would be able to replace me more than adequately. He certainly seemed to have no doubts about the matter.

A few brief words were all that were needed to settle him onto the piano stool and to set his hands in motion. I, meanwhile, took myself off to the sofa, ready to wolf down my fried eggs, one of my favourite foods.

It all seemed so simple, so natural. Soliman had no difficulty in doing the necessary – picking up a discord by ear, fending off the boredom of scales by adding little inflections or a rhythm of his own; he embellished the practice pieces – which I thought were just a bore – with a trill, an arpeggio or an improvised chord.

I was astounded. So was he; clearly thrilled by his hands as if they were no longer part of him. They were agile, inventive and able to reveal something of his inner soul to himself as they made their own way through the music.

*

Now, mornings always had so many surprises in store for me that I would run down early! Musical, tuneful sounds would waft up to delight Miss Boone's ears and she would congratulate me on my hard work and the progress I was making.

'You see, I told you so: you don't get anywhere without hard work.'

Now that she had more confidence in me, she let down her guard and often dozed off in the morning when I was downstairs. Yet she was surprised to see that the marks for music in my report book at the end of each month were still just as poor. She put this down to my piano teacher being cantankerous.

Mademoiselle Petitpas' yellowish skin, according to Miss Boone, showed her disregard for the healthy, sporting life which the English woman advocated and was making every effort to instil in us. Once, having met in the visitors' room at school, they had had words about Napoleon's victories. Mademoiselle Petitpas, a great Bonaparte enthusiast, became tense and whistled through her teeth whilst Miss Boone, not without a certain arrogance, boasted of English victories and lashed out at her three times with the glorious names of Wellington and Waterloo!

'She can't stand me and you're taking the brunt of it!' Miss Boone told me confidentially. 'I'll explain it all to your mother. I'll tell her that you're playing better and better. I'm even toying with the idea of putting you in for a competition. I'll find out if there is one in . . .'

She refrained from saying: '. . . in this God-forsaken country!' Miss Boone was of the opinion that, with the exception of England, everything everywhere else was behind the times and in a mess.

The jaws of the trap were closing in on us. Soon, I knew, I would have to find a way of getting us out of it. For the time being, I was quite satisfied with things as they were. Lulled by the mellifluous tones which I was now beginning to relish, I was taking advantage of some very real nourishment at the same time.

Soliman's playing was getting better and better and he was enjoying it more and more. I occasionally made the effort to teach him a little basic theory or some other pieces within my range. But he seemed to know it all already.

The large open lid of the Pleyel revealed the taut horizontal strings from which floated the tuneful, rippling notes.

The young Sudanese man varied, shaded and punctuated these notes as he improvised more and more freely. Listening to him play, I would nod in time to the beat and tap out the rhythm with my feet. Then, anxious not to arouse Miss Boone's suspicions, he would go back to the painstaking exercises. Soliman saw why, so he said, these had to be done; he was well aware that the flexibility of his wrists and the suppleness of his fingers benefited from such habits of practice.

*

Then, one morning, disaster struck.

Miss Boone was coming down towards us. What had happened? Had she been enthralled by the superb playing? Had she guessed about the switchover? The latter seemed quite out of the question: given her mentality, it would never have dawned on the English woman that such an obvious talent could be tucked away under the dark skin of a servant, destined to remain in profound ignorance.

As chance would have it, we heard her as soon as she set foot on the staircase.

Within a few seconds I had managed to get rid of the tray by dumping it into the frame of the piano and closing the lid down on it. Then, hurriedly, we changed places. Soliman took a duster from his pocket and started to flick at the furniture whilst I tried to make some sense of a sonata that I had not touched in ages.

As I struck the notes, the tray tipped off balance and sent the plateful of half-eaten eggs flying. They then slithered and slipped down between the strings.

Over the next few days – unbeknown to the butler, the housekeeper and the head chef – the young Sudanese man had to spend endless hours making good the damage.

Miss Boone, not having a clue as to what was going on, was wreathed in smiles that morning when she told me that, as a reward for my surprising progress, she was allowing me to have two fried eggs for breakfast instead of the usual porridge.

'Just for once,' she added in her native English.

Normally she was very wary of such food that was, as she put it 'dreadfully bad for the liver' in a scorching hot climate like ours. The governess then explained that she had come down especially to place her order with Soliman before he got our normal 'breakfast' ready in the children's dining room.

'I know how fond you are of fried eggs. In fact, this time you could even have three!'

I had completely lost my appetite for eggs. Nevertheless, I nodded and asked: 'Can my brother have some too?'

'Certainly,' Miss Boone went on. 'Did you know he dived for the first time yesterday?'

Without turning a hair, Soliman, who understood kitchen English, listened to the governess's order of 'Three fried eggs for the children, Soliman. And two boiled eggs for me, with Ceylon tea.'

When the young man had disappeared, Miss Boone said: 'On Sunday, that's tomorrow, I'm taking you and your brother to the Club.'

As a citizen of the British Empire Miss Boone was automatically a member of the very exclusive 'Sporting Club'. She used to drag me down there to play tennis, for which I had only a modicum of talent. She was having more success teaching my younger brother to swim. I can see him now with his curly head and his chubby cheeks, dripping with water and happy. He would pop up all over the pool, splashing the other swimmers and yapping like a puppy-dog.

Afterwards, having let us both loose in the playground where we would hurl ourselves onto the swings, the slides or the see-saw, Miss Boone would go off to the golf course. That was where she met Major White of the Indian Army who had come to spend the first few months of his retirement in Egypt before settling down permanently in England.

Twenty years have passed over these events, these individuals.

It wasn't long before Miss Boone went off to be with her major; they got married and set up house in the county of Gloucestershire. At first we wrote to each other regularly; she embroidered the past in bright colours, rambling on about memories of a happiness I could hardly be said to have shared. I told her about my life in the boarding school, which I quite liked, but also about my constant desire to move far away, to more liberal climes. Gradually we wrote less and less often; soon it was just Christmas cards, which she would pick out with enormous care. Then, nothing. I found out later, through one of their neighbours, that they had both died, three months apart, from the same form of cancer.

Mademoiselle Petitpas, who was over sixty when I was having lessons with her, had gone off Napoleon and taken a fancy to Louis XIV. I was told that she died of old age singing the revolutionary *Marseillaise* beneath a portrait of the Sun King.

My brother, still the sportsman, still impulsive, has had a brilliant career as an international economist.

My own dream became a reality when I came to live in Paris immediately after the war.

As for Soliman, his fate merits a few more words.

It was in the mid-fifties. As I was doing some shopping one afternoon in the arcades round the Palais Royal, my eye was suddenly caught by a little poster stuck onto the door of a nightclub. It showed three faces and I thought one looked familiar. Underneath I saw the name of the pianist: 'Solboy'.

I decided that that night I would go by myself to the club. As soon as I was inside I recognised Soliman at the piano. When he spotted me he bounced up and down several times on his piano stool and waved at me in delight. Over the heads of the large audience he shouted to me in English: 'Wait! Wait! You must wait for me!'

I had no intention of leaving and by dint of waving my arms about I managed to get this across to him straightaway. Then, sitting with a glass of lemonade in front of me, I let myself be bewitched by his syncopated rhythms and his sensitive intonation. I was moved by the music he performed so flawlessly. It fused our own far-off countries and the one where we were at that moment as well as many others. The feeling of well-being that came over me was exquisite.

At two in the morning Soliman came and sat next to me. I hugged him, for I had never been so glad to meet up again with anyone!

'You see,' he said, 'I've got Miss Boone to thank for this. And you too! Let's drink to our secret!'

He went on to tell me that after what those mornings had revealed to him, he had been haunted by his passion for music. After my brother and I had been sent off to our respective boarding schools and after the English woman had left, he had continued to practise every night. So as not to wake my parents, he used to muffle the sound by pressing one of the pedals right down; he had even felt-wrapped the little hammers that struck the strings inside the piano.

A few months later, Soliman had introduced himself to a group of jazz musicians who played at night in one of the capital's big hotels. They hired him immediately and he had gone everywhere with them. He had been living in London for over ten years.

'And what are you doing now?' he asked.

'I write.'

'You write? What sort of thing?'

'The sort of thing we are doing this evening, reminiscing.'

'Do you think that's of any interest?'

'Everything's of interest. It depends on how you spin it out.'

'So you've learnt how to "spin" stories?'

'I try. Occasionally it works, other times, it doesn't.'

'I hope it works this time!' he said giving a loud laugh. 'Will you come and read me your story when it's finished?'

'How long are you in Paris for?'

'Six months.'

'It'll be finished before then. I write in French but I'll translate it.'

'Translate! . . . There you are,' he went on after a few moments, 'music has one advantage; it speaks everybody's language. Don't you sometimes regret giving it up?'

'I was hopeless, don't forget. But when I write, I try, like you, to speak everybody's language.'

'We'll see about that. I can wait.'

'I'll be here one month from now.'

He clapped his hands together: 'You're on. A month from today, at this very table, seven o'clock, for breakfast. I'll bring everything we need. And that morning, I, Soliman, give you my word, that I will make you three of the best fried eggs that you have ever tasted in your life.'

One Day . . . the Enemy

*'Humanity would be cursed if, in order to prove
its courage, it was forced to kill indefinitely.'*
Jean Jaurès

A hot summer Sunday.

Stretching into the distance, for two hundred yards
and more, the roadway was empty. It drank up the sun:
a heavy, white sun glaring down from an ashen sky.

A hot summer Sunday. A day for the shore, for seeking
shade in the pine trees, for saying: 'Hello there, how are
you, how's your wife, your children, your mother, your
uncle? Come in and have a cold drink. Why don't we all
wander down to the beach together . . .' A day for
dreaming, for having a meal under the trees, for taking a
trip up into the mountains, for feeling the air cooling
your lungs as you take each hairpin bend. A time for
laughing, for meeting, for loving one another.

A time for taking your time.

Stretching into the distance, for two hundred yards and
more, the roadway is empty.

Except for two bodies lying in each other's arms.

They are the bodies of two women, lying in a pool of blood which is trickling away and slowly spreading in rivulets across the tarmac.

On either side of this road, the inhabitants of the two communities live face to face in drab grey blocks of flats, four to six storeys high and pocked with bullet holes. These inhabitants, despite the troubles and the bloodshed, have taken the risk of not moving out. Yet they avoid meeting face to face for fear of a confrontation, which neither side wants.

The scarred walls closely frame the closed shutters. Occasionally a window half opens; a head leans out, but pulls back immediately.

The fragment of road, the somnolent block of flats, the shaft of bright light beating down on the two entwined bodies wallowing in a pool of gore – it's just a scene from a film being shown to an audience hidden in the darkness . . . isn't it?

It's just a melodrama thrown up by our imagination and shown simultaneously on every screen across the planet, but the location shot has been set up here – on this precise spot, at this precise moment – by the piercing wail from one of the two women who is howling in the deathly silence.

*

As she listens the old woman can resist no longer. She goes to the window.

It is midday, mealtime. The whole family – all fifteen or so of them, close relatives and cousins – is gathered in the kitchen overlooking a quiet courtyard at the back. Taking advantage of the few minutes that she is alone in the living room – cluttered with mattresses on the floor, littered with blankets and clothes of every kind – the old woman quietly turns the catch.

She pulls the window open towards her, pushes back one flap of the shutters, bends forward and leans out over the street.

It has been months since the bursting shells and crackling of automatic weapons last made any impression on her. Like most of the people in the town, she is used to them now. She has even learnt how to tell the difference between the characteristic sound of one projectile and another; how to tell one gun from another; she can even say where they were made.

With an obvious delight which upsets her, her sons, her grandsons, even her great-grandson, have tried to show her how to handle a firearm.

'To do what with? I'll never use it.'

'Suppose one of us was gunned down in front of you?'

She has no answer to that. She has never felt any hatred. She has always believed, hoped that this land, her land, had been created, long before any others, to fill in the trenches that divide. In its thousand-year history this land has seen so much harmony, so much co-operation, that she is sure it could reinvent them.

'And suppose someone threatened one of us?'

She could not grasp what had happened. The only thing she hated was this madness that had a hold on so many of them, that blindly set one against the other.

'So you'd just let it happen, if we were being murdered?'

No, she would not let it happen. Of course she would not let it happen. But would she use one of these wretched contraptions, if one day . . . ?

'For defence, not to attack.'

'Defence often involves attack. Even in the Bible . . .'

'Don't, don't.'

'So, if they killed someone in your family . . .'

Her family. Who were her family? They were here, down there, everywhere. She used to try to explain, to get down to the roots of the evil. But words were twisted as soon as they were spoken; they could no longer throw light on anything.

'Come on, which side are you on?'

'I don't belong to anyone. I love you all, but I don't belong to you.'

She pulled herself up to her wizened full height. She shook her mass of hair which was still thick and barely beginning to go grey.

She had always felt that she was on the side of those who suffered injustice and violence; there were so many of them in the world. Her green eyes gleamed. A way had to be found to silence the weapons, to make the gesture, to utter the word which . . .

Her family had stopped listening to her. And yet she was not alone in thinking this way, there were others, family, strangers, youngsters, older people. But for some time now it had seemed as if her family, especially her family, were acting as if they had been muzzled. They were closing ranks and communication was becoming impossible.

'Some words have come too late,' they snapped at her.

She repeated: 'Too late . . .'

She went on: 'Never too late.'

And then more quietly, to herself: 'We should have taken more care to keep our eyes open and our hearts alive.'

They gathered round her, patronisingly. One of them held out his gun to her: 'You ought to learn how to use it, you never know . . . You're not scared of it, are you?'

'That would be surprising,' said another. 'You've never been scared of anything!'

She turned away: 'I don't want to.'

It was not that she did not have the nerve, it was . . . How could she explain, how could she explain it to them?

'The others haven't become my enemies . . .'

They were barely listening to her. All around, ears had turned deaf; only voices full of vengeance could make themselves heard.

She would have liked to have given them all a good shake: 'There's been a misunderstanding! Can't you see? Somewhere there's been a misunderstanding.' But as things stood, what good would that do?

Just now, through the walls, the old woman had caught the sound of a burst of gunfire.

The sound was very close. It was going on, no doubt, just below the flats; it was in the roadway; the one which was so often deserted since it had been closed to traffic.

Then, there was silence.

A tangible silence, followed by a wail.

A terrible wail. So excruciating she had clutched at her stomach with both hands as if it had just burst from her own belly.

Often the family would form a circle round her, showing off their guns. They would teach each other how to use them, how to tell a revolver by its handle, a pistol by its butt.

'Look, this part's called the magazine base. That's the breech-block. This is the safety catch. You release it by pressing the catch.'

They were all different ages. They strutted up and down. It was a game. Did they know what the game was?

The redheaded lad, who had just turned nine, was entertaining himself by twirling a revolver on his fore-

127

finger which he had pushed through the trigger guard. He stepped forward and planted himself in front of his grandmother: 'Look, this one hasn't got a cartridge clip, it's got a cylinder.'

Several times he spun the empty cylinder with his bitten thumbnail.

The old woman pulled the child close to her, whispered in his ear, trying to explain to him what this object really was, what he might well become . . .

The little lad wriggled out of her arms, slipping the revolver out of his little hands into his grandmother's.

'Here you are. Touch it.'

'No, I don't want to.'

She tried to talk to him again; to tell him about death, to strip bare the appalling masquerade.

Peevishly, the child walked off.

Just now, when they had all gone back into the kitchen, the old woman had recognised the continuous crackle of an automatic weapon. It was most probably one of those light machine guns used for close combat. A paramilitary unit had probably infiltrated the district and one of them had just fired off all his rounds.

If it had been any other day, the old woman would have joined her family for lunch, had that wail not made her jump.

That interminable, keening wail.

*

The old woman pulls the window open towards her. Then, pushing back one flap of the shutters, leans out over the street.

There, in the centre of the roadway, her arms and legs splayed out beneath her billowing yellow skirt, a woman is lying on her back. She is bleeding profusely. All around her the tarmac is bright red; the scarlet slick spreads and spreads.

A second woman sits astride the first. Her legs and knees grip the thighs of the one on the ground.

The upper part of her body is resting on the other's chest, her face is pressed to hers. Their dark hair tangles together. For a moment, you might think that the second woman has also been shot were it not for the fact that, every so often, she lifts her head to continue her wailing, broken by: 'Kill me. Kill me too.'

That blue dress with its red polka dots, the old woman has seen it before, here, in the neighbourhood. Who was wearing it? Who's that woman wailing?

Arms, many arms, more and more arms are already tugging at the grandmother, pulling her away. Hard, firm arms are grasping her elbows, her shoulders, her waist, forcing her to move back.

The old woman won't give in. The soles of her shoes drag along the tiles of the floor. But the others outnumber her and are stronger than her. Inevitably, she slides slowly back inside the living room.

'I want to go down into the street. I want to go and see . . .'

'You're mad!'

The family close the shutters, pull the window shut and double lock it.

At that very moment, a French window opens a crack on the first floor of the block opposite.

A little girl, hair tied up in a large black plait, creeps out onto the balcony.

The stone balustrade is high; the child climbs onto the plinth, puts her hands on the coping and pushes her head between the balusters.

Like nearly all the inhabitants of this town, the little girl has already seen death. She has already seen blood; but never at such close quarters.

There, just there, beneath the balcony. A red puddle oozes out round these two women, bound one to the other. The one on top occasionally lifts her head to let out a terrifying wail.

Wide eyed, the little girl stares at the scene. She recognises the one who is wailing: it's Ammal, a distant relative. The little girl is cold, her hands tighten on the coping, her knees are trembling.

*

Suddenly, behind her, she hears footsteps. Her mother's, her older sisters', the young maid's, her cousins'? . . . She doesn't want to know. She doesn't turn round. She will not go back inside. She scampers away as fast as her legs will carry her.

Arms try to catch hold of her. She gets away from them. Her plait whips across her back. She runs in all directions, scuttling from one end of the balcony to the other. She slams into the corners, ricochets against the glass panels of the French window and careers into the walls and the stone partition.

As she dashes here and there and fights for breath, she sees in her mind's eye the large white hen whose head has just been cut off . . . it was in the country, last winter. A bubbling, crimson stream spurts up from the little creature's neck. The decapitated hen hurtles into obstacles, rushes backwards and forwards, legs and wings flying, and finally collides with the steps to the house, scattering red spots onto the earth and onto the treads.

In the end, hands had closed around it.

Now they're closing in from all directions on her too. Now they're grabbing hold of her. There's no point in struggling.

'I want to see. Leave me alone!'

They clamp their arms right round the little girl and carry her off into the house.

The shutters slam. The windows close.

They even go as far as to push a large wardrobe in front of the French windows.

Bazooka and mortar fire pound incessantly. Shells and rockets rain down on the town. Relentlessly, one death follows another . . .

Five blocks of flats – three on one side, two on the other – flank the two hundred metres of roadway where there's not a car to be seen.

A scorching sun lights up the deserted street, makes it look like a corner of a bullring set for a scene from *Death in the Afternoon*.

In various parts of this town, tragedy strikes, catching in its trap a human being here, a living soul there. Like a large, sprawling body, the whole city is breathless, crumbling, dying; sweeping the masses along in its own faceless destruction.

As it moves in concentric circles, spreading across the whole planet, overrunning the whole of History past and future, violence is relentlessly pulling life apart. A few individuals it snatches up in its talons, letting their names drop as fodder for the history books; but the majority it flings into deepest oblivion.

Being particularly vulnerable to missiles, the upper floors have been deserted. Families have taken refuge in the apartments lower down and have even begun to make use of their cellars.

These lower floors are full to bursting! Overcrowded with whole families, both close and extended. Families, encumbered with words, with petty irritation, with tenderness; families with their tentacular, loving arms. Arms that bind, embrace, protect, invade, enslave.

Flabby arms with broad purple veins, young arms, cosseting and smooth, muscular arms covered in fine down. Arms to go round waists, to go round shoulders; arms to draw you down into the shelter of the corridors and the cellars where you wait, in the warm, comforted by the reassuring presence of others nearby. Whilst outside the madness rages, with its shrieks, its explosions and its fires!

Wide open. The neighbours have opened their doors wide open; they too have always been part of her close family. Before the hostilities, the walls were no barrier, one set of lives flowed into another. A fit of temper, an argument; these were talked about, passed from person to person, exaggerated; they quickly spread right round the block. Hearsay mingled with certainty, wicked lies mingled with kindness. A birth would eclipse a death, a marriage would alleviate a disaster.

They are generous, warm, supportive; but families are often voracious, fortified by their surroundings! They are hospitable, helpful, kindly; but families are often entangled in binding and intolerant roots; families can suddenly bond in the interests of dark and complex causes.

The family, tender, serene, a part of you; and yet terrifying at one and the same time.

Following that wail, that howl, the young woman had once more bent down over her companion's body.

Her back, at first shaken by sobs, had suddenly taken on a corpse-like rigidity. But it was not she who was injured. It was from the body of her companion alone that the stream of blood flowed continuously, turning brown as it spread across the tarmac.

The injured woman's legs, exposed as far as her knees, splayed beneath her festive yellow skirt. Barely a few minutes ago, what celebration was she on her way to? Where was she going before this hail of bullets tore into her, spraying in one burst her back, her shoulders and her neck?

The volley had been so rapid that she had collapsed before the look on her face – joyful and confident – could change.

The other one, who had been coming to meet her, had dashed forward to catch her as she fell.

But the body had slipped from her arms.

So she had thrown herself down onto her companion.

Ammal is wearing the blue dress with red polka dots which, just now, the grandmother leaning out of her window had recognised. She and the old woman lived in the same district, they often talked to each other, they understood each other. While the hostilities had been going on, although they belonged to different communities, they had tried to meet up again.

Panic-stricken, Ammal looks into the dying face.

'Carry on . . . swear to me . . . that you . . . will carry on . . .'

Vera's lips freeze around these last words, around her open mouth.

Cradling the head in both arms, Ammal lifts it up. Feverishly, she clasps it to her, she rocks it, she strokes it like a tiny child she is comforting with her tenderness, her breath, her words, with every part of her physical being.

With mounting apathy, the face becomes vacant, grows cold.

It was then that the wail took hold of the young survivor.

Reaching deep into every fibre of her body, stretching the muscles of her neck, filling her throat, stiffening the nape of her neck, the wail takes complete possession of her.

Rooted deep in the moans and lamentations of her ancestors, this mighty, resonant, dizzying wail delays and denies, for a few moments more, the unbearable fact.

The young woman surrenders herself to this strange,

wild voice rising from all the woes of the world.

Around her, everything reels.

The city crushed by the civil war is gone. Gone are the houses, gone are the families, gone are the dead, gone is the future, gone are the dreams, gone is the ashen face . . .

All that is left is this tiny island of tarmac spinning in the void!

All that remains is this island against which, like foaming waves, hopes and despair, loves and hate, crash down and die.

Consumed by this wail, there is nothing left of this young woman but her throat. Nothing but an unbroken sound.

Her ears are deaf, her eyes are blind. She does not even notice the little girl on the balcony opposite, who has pushed her head through the stone balusters and who is staring at her, terror-stricken.

Fear vanishes; the wail inures against it. In this open space, exposed to danger, to reprisals, Ammal lets herself be carried along, lets herself be wrapped up in this howl from which, from time to time, the same nerve-shattering words escape: 'Kill me! Kill me too!'

It was only later, when the wail had left her, that the young woman realised she was helpless, weak, a bundle of grief.

For weeks they had been preparing, eagerly and meticulously, for this meeting. This meeting, planned to the last detail, was to give events a new twist.

But within the space of a few seconds, everything had shattered.

Everything had collapsed, within the space of a few seconds!

Ammal leant forward once more. Once more her cheek lay against the now cold cheek, her long brown hair indistinguishable from the dark hair clotted with blood.

Stunned, beyond tears, the young woman is on the verge of fainting.

'What's your name?'

'Ammal. What's yours?'

'Vera.'

The play area is on a slope. The two little girls hare down it, chasing a ball bouncing over the stones.

'Here you are. Have it.'

'Keep it. You have it.'

To get back to their friends they walk up the slope together, hand in hand. Their dark hair flutters on their shoulders. They run, they laugh beneath the pines. Everywhere there are views of the sea.

'Do you go to the beach much?'

'Sometimes.'

They ask each other questions, lots of questions; the

playful, the serious questions of childhood.

'Has your God got a different name from mine?'

'I think it's the same. Or else he doesn't exist.'

'That's what I think, too.'

They are seven, ten, twelve . . . They swap combs, exercise books, mirrors.

They are getting on for thirteen, fifteen. They take prejudices and customs in their stride. They push against barriers; sometimes it just needs a little shove for a prejudice here, a custom there, to come tumbling down amid their own clouds of dust. The days stretch out; the months roll past. They keep their eyes open, they leave the nice districts behind them, they venture into different ones. They see corrugated-iron huts, doors made out of pieces of cardboard, gaggles of children wallowing in muddy puddles, women who have no life, adolescents who have no future. They feel ashamed; they feel the pain. They want answers, from each other, from anyone. They devour books and newspapers. They are not alone.

They are sixteen . . . they make a pact against all forms of discrimination, restriction, division, humiliation.

'You won't change, will you?'

'Never. Later on, if you see me changing, you must tell me.'

'Of course. You too.'

*

They are seventeen, eighteen. They swap books, dresses. Their breasts are smaller than their mothers', their thighs longer. They talk a lot about love. They cope with it uneasily, passionately, somewhere between freedom and repression. They fascinate boys; they unsettle the lads.

Months pass. Weeks pass. They take exams. They work. They creep onwards; they leap onwards. They confide in their grandmothers; some veiled, others not. They listen to their encouragement or their scolding, but at least they listen. They shock both their mothers, the over-submissive one and the one who merely wastes her time on pretty clothes and showing off. They confront their fathers; when a chink appears, they slip through it. What is going on elsewhere is stimulating, it makes waves, it creates excitement. People are communicating.

Barricades and chasms are not always found where people say they are; sometimes they have nothing to do with place or age. Some minds suffer from anxiety, others create it. Time is on the move, rich in events. These are times when life can be lived to the full.

But one morning, everything was smashed to pieces.

One bloodbath unleashed another.

As if every corner of this town overflowed with them, guns of all calibres appeared from nowhere. An arsenal of instruments of war rose to the surface of the earth.

Very quickly, all these weapons took a hold of the town, trapping it in a malevolent circle that no words, no sign of peace could penetrate.

One massacre was the excuse for another. Each gunman felt himself inspired, all-powerful, vested with a mission. The evil spell spread throughout the generations. A gun bestowed authority, strength, power. What words could banish it or overcome its tyranny?

Guns were the law. Men and women, held in the sway of these weapons, fascinated by them, seduced by the intoxication of death, allowed themselves to be carried away in a macabre whirlwind.

Barricades, street battles, fires all followed in quick succession. One atrocity avenged another. Terrifying stories circulated of the sick being pulled from their beds and executed in front of other patients; women raped surrounded by their children; old people shot, corpses desecrated, the injured dragged behind cars . . .

On both sides, the more tolerant, distraught by their bereavements, caught up in their pain, retreated into their original factions and demanded revenge.

There were more and more reprisals. The other side lost all its distinguishing features only to be replaced by one single, grimacing mask, capable of any abomination. Stupid, cruel generalisations were made; excuses were found, but only for kith and kin.

Within a short time, the town split into two opposing camps.

*

And yet, hope lingered on in the minds of a few; a trickle of water, hidden underground, stubbornly flowed beneath the scorched, arid land. Telephone calls, secret talks, persistently mended the persistently broken ties.

One morning, a plea from an amateur radio operator had brought 70,000 people from the two communities onto the streets. Shoulder to shoulder, demanding an end to this suicidal struggle, they had marched though the town, applauded by the onlookers.

But, since then, the piles of corpses had grown high.

Since then, people's hearts had grown heavy.

This meeting had been carefully prepared over several weeks. Ammal and Vera, who had not seen each other for more than a year, were to walk towards each other to meet again, here, on this patch of roadway so like a boulevard.

On meeting, the two young women were to join hands and to shout out to the people in the surrounding buildings to come down and join them.

At that very moment, lookouts – in place since the early hours, ready for this meeting – would be passing on the information. It would be picked up immediately and sent on to other eagerly waiting friends.

In increasing numbers, people would come out of their homes. Tired of the bloodshed and the desolation, a multitude of them were, no doubt, just waiting for a signal to converge; someone would guide them towards this open space and from there they would go down, en masse, into the town to demand an end to the killing.

Like rivulets heading towards a delta, the countless twisting lanes – steep, narrow and running one into another – wove a net which converged and tightened around this broad roadway. The very fact that there were so many meant that this open space could be reached from everywhere, before the forces of discord found out and managed to stem the gathering crowd.

In a few moments, everything will begin.

Ammal has just appeared in the distance, at one end of the street.

Vera at the other.

From a distance they wave, hesitantly.

Now they are moving toward each other to the middle of the road, both at the same moment.

They are walking, easily, in their espadrilles which can be seen below the yellow skirt and below the blue dress with its red polka-dots.

With nerves at breaking point, borne along by an excitement which is a blend of elation and fear, joy and trepidation, they move forward, one step after the other, like acrobats on a tightrope.

Beneath the overarching white sun, they move forward, step by step; their temples throb, their breath quivers, their muscles tense.

As if in an open-air circus, they walk toward a fixed spot, right in the middle of the ring.

But soon, abruptly, there will be those bursts of machine-gun fire.

The massive front doors of one of the nearby blocks of flats has just opened a crack.

Holding the little redhead's revolver in front of her, the old woman comes out of the shadow and moves onto the street.

What trick has she used to escape? She does not know herself. She just knows that she has to be quick. Upstairs, in a flash, once she had remembered Ammal, she had understood the whole thing. She would go and save her herself. She will not let this shred of hope vanish.

'I'm on my way, lass!'

The old woman hurries towards the pile of clothes which is now all that can be seen of the two young women; hurries towards this suddenly motionless heap.

On the edge of the pavement she takes off her mauve felt slippers; their flapping soles would slow her down.

She moves forward, her feet bare on the tarmac.

'I'm on my way, lass!'

*

Keeping her eyes open, the old woman glances around, searching. Whoever might have wanted to shoot Ammal would have to face her, gun in hand. She blesses her great-grandson's perseverance in showing her how to use it.

The old woman moves forward inch by inch. She no longer feels the stiffness in her knees, the weakness in her fingers. She is inching along. She is getting there.

She has hatred in her sights.

In the distance, the whine of an ambulance can be heard.

Then silence once more.

Step by step, the old woman is moving forward. She doesn't know if she will get to where she is going. If someone, at that precise moment, is taking aim at her back, between the shoulders . . . She is vigilant. She will do her best. If the young woman is threatened, she'll pull the trigger. Then, and only then, will her aim be true.

'I'm on my way, lass!'

Just a few yards more!

On the balcony opposite, a stubborn little girl has come back. Her head is thrust between the balusters. She knows Ammal, she remembers the other young woman. Suddenly, she too sees the whole thing.

She spots the old woman; she gives a nod in her direction.

When the grandmother is really close, the little girl unties the green satin ribbon which is wound round her thick plait, and throws it to her, like an offering, over the balustrade.

All of a sudden the elderly heart takes fire. Later, if she is still alive, she will pick up the ribbon.

Her pace quickens. The old woman pushes on and on, she is getting nearer.

Surely people will open their windows, will come running out . . .

The Door Across the Street

For over fifteen years I'd managed to live without paying any attention to the door, without even noticing it. Then one day I was struck by its presence.

Perhaps it was because it was so ordinary – it's just like the doors on all the other buildings, down to the last detail – that it had, until then, escaped my curiosity.

Suddenly, there it was. Set back slightly between walls darkened by age, it merely made up part of the narrow street – my street – which cars shunned in the midst of the buzzing, frenetically swirling hive of the city. It's a gully of a street where, at times, the roofs merge with the lowering sky. There it was, this door, throwing the dreary stretch of concrete out of kilter, as it were, and forcing me to look at it.

Beyond it, empty space. It appears to lead nowhere; or rather, it does lead somewhere; to a minute area which, from the outside, might make you think of a little court-yard. A courtyard where, as far as I know, no one has ever ventured. No gap, I should imagine, has ever appeared around this door; no one, when I've been about, has ever tried to open it.

Both my rooms overlook it. I gaze at it from my first-floor flat. I gaze at it for minutes on end, wondering why the fact that it's there fascinates and intrigues me. Then I stop wondering and let myself be carried away.

Shortly after spotting it, I caught myself standing there, rooted to the pavement in front of it.

I took in its knots and its roughness; I examined all its different colours, I counted the scars left on its surface by the passing years and the rain. I lay the palms of my hands on it. With the tip of my forefinger I meandered over its panels, rough here, smooth there.

As for my flat, well, these days I'm neglecting it more and more. I don't even put flowers out now. I make no attempt to make it look nice; that view of the door is all I need.

'Soon,' I say to myself, 'I'll cross the road, I'll open the door, I'll go in, I'll see! . . .'

There are times when I feel that doing it would be natural and easy. Yet I'm forever putting off making up my mind until tomorrow.

Jean understood me immediately when I told him about the door; but I found it far more difficult getting him to really look at it.

As we leant, elbow to elbow, on the windowsill, he

was only interested in the neighbouring buildings and the parked cars . . . Very soon he got tired of the street, dived back into the room and, almost impatiently, called me back inside.

Sitting close to each other, we talked at length – about anything but the door. I tried to steer the conversation back to it, I would have liked it to still be a part of us; I would also perhaps have liked to ask Jean for his help and advice. But the longer we talked – drifting from one topic to another – the further the door faded from sight, like a raft washed away on an ocean of words.

I got the feeling that, if I persisted, it would crumble up as it rose in my throat, and dissolve in my saliva before ever reaching my tongue and taking shape as a word. Afraid of losing it completely, I gave up trying to squeeze it into the discussion. I even went further; in order to keep it by me somewhere and, in a way, to save it, I swallowed it all in one go; I gulped it down whole into the depths of my very being.

'What have you been up to this week?' Jean asked.

He then reeled off the arrangements for his new business. His ideas grew like a construction kit with its securely tightened bolts and its close-fitting hinges.

I admired him. He talked effortlessly.

Rain is spattering the door. Once again, standing on the pavement, I'm looking at it closely.

It has no handle, no bell, no lock, no knocker. There

is nothing to indicate that it might be locked on the inside. On the contrary, it seems to invite an elbow, a hand or even just a fingertip to give it a friendly little push.

But I don't want to try anything yet. I'm afraid that one false move now and I might have to use force later on. And that I must not do, not at any cost.

All last night I grappled with its ghost.

My gaze turned to steel and bore into its timbers. I went stubbornly on like that indomitable insect, the woodworm. I thought I had arrived at its core, but then I found myself flowing down a seam, straying along a splinter, avoiding the gnarled patches, crossing a layer of veneer, coming up a fibre only to fan out instantly through shafts and runnels or to lose my way in a crack.

Undeterred, I started over again.

One groove would reveal another. I would plunge into a world which was more and more blind, more and more just wood.

A few days later, I decided I would work my way round the obstacle.

I had noticed that to one side of the door the foot of the wall was crumbling. Like a taut patch of fabric, the render had burst in places; rough pebbles, bonded with some sort of black stuff, were threatening to come away.

'I ought to loosen a few of these stones,' I said to

myself, 'and dig out an opening I can get through.'

I waited for night time, I waited for the street to be empty, I waited for winter.

A thin layer of snow levelled off the paving stones. I trod as lightly as I could so as not to spoil all that whiteness; despite my efforts, each step left a smear on the ground.

I was wearing a warm, jersey tracksuit which fitted well and didn't hamper any of my movements. Over that, a raincoat.

With one knee on the ground, hemmed in by the cold and the dark, I started by scraping away at the spot using a spade.

The small patches of cement flaked off easily. The gravel lining gave way. I picked up handfuls of it and filled the pockets of my tracksuit, then the ones in my raincoat; soon they were full to bursting. I was feeling more and more cheerful and made up my mind to come back the following evening armed with a shopping bag.

I went back. The wall went on parting with its stones. Very soon I needed a bigger bag, then a bucket. Finally I needed my neighbour's worn-out old pram which she lent me without a word.

Each time my load got heavier. Yet the way through was no clearer.

*

I carried on, working until I was out of breath. Bit by bit I was caught up in the sheer pleasure of my little game. Uncovering the stonework, freeing it from its cement cage, collecting it up, then looking for a place to get rid of it; for a while I found it all more satisfying than I could ever have hoped.

The dustbins nearby weren't big enough now. In the end, on the banks of the river – which wasn't far from my part of town – I found a deserted patch of land. I trudged back and forth in the night, straining my shoulders and my arms against the pram as I pushed it towards the river's edge.

After a few months I had to accept the fact: the mound on the riverbank was growing a little higher each evening, but to the left of the door the hole was getting no bigger.

I trained my torch on it. The opening was still tiny; you could have plugged it with a baby's fist.

However, the heap on the riverbank was reassuring. During the day I would walk smugly round it, or else gaze at it from the top of the parapet. I had got it to look like a pyramid and I made sure that – despite its crumbling slopes – it retained its pointed shape. The sight of this pile convinced me that my efforts were something real; whenever I saw it my enthusiasm flared up again.

One night, my hard work gave me a tremendous

boost: amongst one of the loads I discovered a pebble completely encrusted in moss.

One summer morning, standing at my window, I caught sight of some tourists taking photos of the door.

Women wearing flowing, colourful dresses were posing in front of it. The men, in their shirtsleeves, their jackets tied round their waists, took the shots and printed them immediately. They were all speaking a language I couldn't understand a single word of. I wondered if they were talking about the door and how it was showing up on their photos.

I hurried down to try and slip into their group and find out why, despite its perfectly ordinary appearance, it was that particular door which they had chosen to want to remember.

But already they were moving off. In a flurry of gestures and voices they disappeared, whisked out of sight at the first turning.

I was alone again.

Later on, I tried to get my son interested in the door.

He's got pitch-black hair like pure ink; his ears stick out, making him look as if he's on the *qui vive*, as if he's listening to what's happening elsewhere.

One afternoon, after he'd got home from school, I pointed the door out to him and he immediately suggested climbing over it.

He failed; the surface of the wall gave no footing, no support.

So he suggested throwing his ball over the lintel. I said yes and he did it there and then.

The yellow ball soared up in an elegant curve before disappearing, so we thought, into the courtyard.

Then, straight away, back it came, describing an inimitable arc and falling at our feet.

'I'm going to do it again!'

'Later.'

'Why?'

I didn't know what to say.

'Let me do it again!'

I managed to talk him out of it. I could sense that he was one of those people who would be fascinated by the risks involved. I wanted to stop him getting tied up too soon with solving the riddle. He was so very young, I wanted to put off the moment.

I also had a vague feeling that there was a way of settling this which was more straightforward and yet, at the same time, more complicated. But I was still far from having a clue as to what it was.

My son, skipping in time to his ball, went off with barely a second thought.

*

On the other hand, there are times when I get the impression that I ought to be even more determined in my hunt for a way through; I feel that chanting, dancing and madness would prise this place open for me, that they would, finally, make the meaning of the door clear to me; perhaps clarify the meaning of where I was going and of what the universe was all about.

Although I feel that everything in my life is all I could wish for, I cannot get rid of this pain. Or is it pleasure? . . . Often I'm even afraid that the hours I've wasted might gradually make that most painful, most basic of secrets inaccessible to me.

So, overcome by impatience, I can see myself hurrying across the road, throwing myself against the door and tackling it head on.

I hammer at it with my fists. I hack at it with my axe. I make very short work of it.

Once I am on the other side I can see myself finding that it is quite empty, except for an empty laugh. An empty laugh . . . which would be, perhaps, nothing but my own echo.

The other week, a woman in a hat stood herself in front of the door.

Standing on tiptoe, she seemed to be looking for some writing. When she'd finished, she turned round and, spotting me at my window, shouted up at me. The street was empty, making her voice sound particularly shrill.

'Is this number 7?' she shouted, jabbing her finger towards the stone doorpost on the right. 'Where's the plaque gone?'

'No, number 7 is on your left.'

'Oh, right! It's number 5.'

'Number 5 is on your right.'

'What?'

I explained: 'It's between numbers 5 and 7.'

'Do you mean it's number 6?'

'No, the even numbers are opposite. Number 6 is this one, the house I'm in.'

'So it's 5a then?'

'That's not possible,' I told her confidently. 'That door has nothing to do with any of the others.'

'Oh! . . .'

She stared at me suspiciously.

'What number are you looking for?' I asked.

'111.'

'111 is much further up, well past the place de l'Eglise.'

'I know,' she cut in. 'I know that! But I can't abide what I can't understand.'

I smiled. She glared at me as if she held me personally responsible for her discomfiture.

She went away, her body lurching forward as if it were made out of thousands of badly greased axles. Her high-arched shoes hammered the ground.

I could imagine the tarmac bursting into tiny, painful stars beneath her heels.

*

At the moment, everything in my room faces the door.

I've arranged the furniture so that it looks like a shoal of little fishing smacks bobbing on the tide until the wind gets up. Bit by bit, all the objects which fill the room have come to look as if they were designed and produced for this one, peculiar purpose.

Often, too, things lose their solidity; then I feel as if there's a swarm of arrows, ready to strike an invisible target, just waiting for the signal from the archer slumbering within me before they take to the air!

I have just hung up that long mirror – the one I avoid looking into because the only objects in it that can see me are my own eyes – at the right height at the far end of the room. So, no matter where I am, it catches the reflection of the door and bowls it back to me.

There are moments when I have the feeling the door is being covered over in layers of plaster and that I'm standing helplessly by as the walls either side eat away at it.

Even though I'm a martyr to fits of acute anxiety at such times, I've never given up hope of one day seeing the door reappear and of finding the way through.

True, I often have to put up with times when I'm miserable and bewildered.

But not a soul, no, not one single soul, should ever dare take it into their head to stop me fretting about it.

The Ancestor and His Donkey

For Bernard Giraudeau

Astride his grey donkey, with his baggy, rusty black trousers gathered in at the ankles, his feet in yellowish leather babouches which were constantly slipping off his heels, a long-sleeved coarse cotton shirt flapping under his flannel waistcoat and a red fez slightly askew on his greying hair; this was how, in the 1860s, the ancestor had roamed the souks of old Cairo, selling his corks. On either side of his mount hung two sacks, full to bursting.

Still unmarried at over thirty, Assad had not long left his native Lebanon. It had looked as if there was going to be a famine. The tribal and sectarian struggles – which lead to the occasional massacre, then to long-term vendettas – blighted any relationships. Being completely devoid of the hatred and the clannishness his family was trying to impose on him, he decided to go into exile.

Taking with him several bales of cork harvested from the bark of local oaks, he set off on a sailing ship en route for Alexandria.

As soon as he set foot on foreign soil, Assad felt a sudden surge of creativity which, until then, he had

lacked. He went off to the capital, easily found some-
where to live and bought a donkey, which he called
Saf-Saf. These nonsense syllables sounded affectionate
and feisty and had sprung to his lips of their own accord.
From that day on, Saf-Saf had been his shop, his means
of transport and his confidant.

His business concerns became child's play. The more
corks he whittled in all shapes and sizes, the more he
came up with new ideas. He took as much delight in
meeting other traders, visiting their tiny shops, swapping
bits of news and joking over a cup of coffee as he did
in treating them, out of a bulbous jar hanging from his
saddle, to mulberry cordial served in a pewter beaker
which he buffed up with a chamois leather.

In his home village, the people – hospitable too, but
more boastful, more pretentious than the people here –
had reduced him to a diffident silence. Unlike there, he
felt at ease here amongst these Egyptians. They were
generally poor, but cheerful and kind.

Whenever business went on too long Saf-Saf would
bray and kick the ground with his hooves, stirring up
clouds of dust. Assad would calm him down with some
of the lumps of sugar that filled his pockets. On other
occasions, as a treat, he would garland his neck with
several strings of blue beads designed to ward off the evil
eye. This was a superstition in which, amongst others,
Assad did not particularly believe.

In the evenings, with his donkey in the room they
shared looking out onto an evil-smelling cul-de-sac, he

would make it up to the animal by stroking him and talking to him about their day: 'Saf-Saf, my brother, what would I do without you? Our business is doing so well that I've run out of cork already. I'll have to get a whole lot sent out from my old village. It won't be long 'til I double your oat ration. I'll buy myself a new waistcoat and some more trousers.'

Content with life, Assad could think of no better way to spend the money he earned.

It was then that a fellow Christian came on the scene. This man – who had left the Lebanon twenty years previously – ran a goldsmith's business in Cairo and offered him an investment opportunity.

'An investment?'

'You let me have a sum of money, and I swear by Saint Anthony I'll turn it into a gold mine for you! Before very long, I'll give you back twice, perhaps even three times as much!'

The goldsmith did not know how right he was. Gratefully, Assad handed him the money which was burning a hole in his pocket and which he was on the brink of giving away to all and sundry. The man bought him a plot of land in the suburbs which was being sold by a Turk whose business was in trouble.

In no time at all, the value of the plot rose tenfold. Armed with the right papers, and making a huge profit on each transaction, the goldsmith sold the property on and immediately reinvested the money, buying other plots further out. And so on and so on. Until the day when Assad and he found themselves owners of several hundred thousand hectares, worth an absolute fortune.

Unaware of how his investments were flourishing, Assad went on quietly doing what he had always done.

On the evening he heard the staggering news, he had the feeling that someone had just thrown an enormous boulder into the peaceful lake of his existence!

From then on, he pondered over what attitude he should take. He could no longer ignore the situation or his newfound status. His neighbours and, above all, the members of his own community – with whom he had never really had much to do, preferring to mix with the locals – made it their duty to remind him.

His fellow countrymen overwhelmed him with their marks of respect. Harping on about their shared roots, they discovered, most opportunely, innumerable family ties with him. They advised him to settle down as soon as he could, boasting that they could find him a bride from the same background: a Christian girl, and one only just reaching puberty at that. Every family had a daughter in stock for him. Assad was getting on for forty – a fair old age in those days; it was imperative that he should start thinking about producing a good number of children to be his future heirs.

That evening Saf-Saf wouldn't stop braying despondently. Sugar, oats and stroking all failed to settle him down. He gazed at his master with his huge brown eyes misted over with sadness, as if he had a premonition of a sombre future for them both.

He was not wrong.

Overnight, Assad found himself the owner of enormous cotton plantations which were rented out to small farmers. Other tracts of land were waiting to be put to profitable use.

Aboard some of the first trains to run in Egypt, Assad took Saf-Saf with him every time he went off to this far-flung part of the countryside. They spent many a long week there, recapturing the pleasure of walking and trading as in the past.

Fields took the place of souks, sandy tracks replaced alleyways, canals with their muddy waters were vaguely reminiscent of the great Nile as it flows through the capital.

When he shared the peasants' meals with them at the foot of a tree, listened to their grievances and promised to put them right, visited them in their shacks and invited them onto the terrace of his home, having killed a sheep in their honour, Assad felt almost the same vitality and cheerfulness as in the past when he used to wander through the old town.

When he mixed with these men, Assad felt himself far less a fish out of water – for his wealth seemed so much like a disguise that it made him uncomfortable. As Saf-Saf carried him around or trotted along at his side, he would gaily shake his tail to chase away the flies and nod his head cheerfully to make the rows of beads jangle.

This happiness could not last!

His green-eyed wife, the buxom Asma, first the mother to one son, then two, then three . . . rapidly came to dominate her husband.

The in-laws prided themselves on coming from sound stock. They bragged of estates, possessions, lost alas in the internecine struggles which had wrought havoc in their native country and forced them into exile. For all these reasons, the family tribe considered that, having agreed to let one of their daughters wed beneath herself by marrying a 'cork salesman', it was not in a position to make any further concessions. They referred to Assad's simplicity as childishness: 'After all,' they said, 'he has chosen a donkey as his best friend!'

His attitude could not help but mislead these boorish peasants whom he treated as his family. If left in his incompetent hands, the farms would go to wrack and ruin. It was, therefore, their duty to look after the well-being of Asma and the 'little darlings' who were being born one after the other and to render the fellow harmless: 'He is so ignorant that he signs the bottom of documents with a cross and his thumbprint.'

They begged Assad – intimidating him with legalistic arguments – to give up spending time in the country so he could devote himself exclusively to exporting cotton and sugar cane. They would soon have some offices set up in the city. He would manage them, backed up – it went without saying – by two of his brothers-in-law and Uncle Naïm. This Uncle Naïm, a tyrannical old man, had been promoted to the rank of 'patriarch' after the death of his older brother, Asma's father.

The white Italianate villa with its marble porch, its colonnades and its balconies had more than twenty rooms.

It was surrounded by a large garden. A bower of hollyhock, constantly green grass, clumps of rhododendrons, beds of roses, gladioli and chrysanthemums, herbaceous borders of nasturtiums or pansies, were all maintained on a permanent basis by three efficient gardeners.

But there just weren't enough trees. Only one, the banyan – already on the site when they built the house – had been saved by the architect. It stood in the east of the garden perched on its many roots. Its gnarled, ancient branches gave shade for Saf-Saf.

'I don't want that ridiculous animal roaming round the house where the guests might see it,' grumbled Asma.

At the end of a rope – which Assad had made sure he had let out as far as it would go – the captive donkey, pretending to have forgotten this imposition, trotted round and round the tree whenever the fancy took him.

As soon as he spotted his master, Saf-Saf stood slap in front of him and gazed at him lovingly. To earn his forgiveness, Assad was giving him bigger and bigger rations of oats, sugar and hugs.

There were certain decisions on which Assad would never compromise. Whatever his family might think, he was going to keep Saf-Saf with him forever. He let others get on with their lives, but he insisted on having his own way of life and he was going to hold on to it.

He had a cell-like bedroom built at the end of a long, narrow corridor leading to the main part of the house. It was whitewashed and contained just one bed, a chair and a table. Pinned to the wall, a yellowing photograph of himself astride his donkey – lugging his 'cork sacks' – reminded him of a past which was unclouded and happy.

A French window opened onto the banyan tree. From every corner of his room Assad could see both the donkey and the tree.

Asma labelled this protuberance 'an obnoxious wart which mars our noble abode'.

Several times a day, as he was setting off to go to it, Assad would call out: 'I'm off to get my breath of fresh air. See you later!'

Not being too good at business and thinking of his children's interests – despite three miscarriages Asma had already presented him with eight – Assad had willingly entrusted all financial matters to members of his wife's family.

In their hands, the fortune grew. Signs of the fact were

everywhere; more domestic staff were taken on, an Austrian governess then an Albanian coachman arrived, the receptions became more and more lavish, there was an annual subscription to a box at the opera. All of which put his family in the ranks of those who mattered, gave them an entrée into 'high society' and lead them to hope that their descendents would marry into class and money.

When they were very small Assad's children had been fascinated by this whimsical father of theirs, but gradually let themselves be seduced by their mother's family and the practical benefits it brought them.

Some of them later criticised their father for not doing anything to help the family rise in the world and for taking great delight in conjuring up memories which could hardly be said to be distinguished.

They stopped taking any interest in Saf-Saf, they stopped stroking him, feeding him or climbing on his back. Seeing them on the other side of the lawn he would bray in vain to attract their attention.

It was not his family's ambitions which bothered Assad; what hurt him, even exasperated him was their posing, and that insufferable pretentiousness of theirs.

Being conscious of his own lack of education, he made a serious effort to do something about it.

The schoolmaster, hunchbacked, short-sighted old Hazan, paid him a visit three times a week. He would shuffle across the garden with his canvas bag stuffed full of books tucked under his arm. Before going into his pupil's room, he would stroke Saf-Saf for quite some time and slip a honey cake between his teeth.

Assad learnt to read and to write; he was attentive and quick. After each lesson, Hazan would chant a poem to him.

If then you can render me a service, I will show myself not unworthy of it; but if that is not your practice, I will, just the same, say: I thank you.

The intelligent man,
having laid bare all the goods of this world to examine
them
will find they become in the end
an enemy dressed as a friend.

'That is by Abou Nawass,' he murmured to Assad, 'the rebellious poet with the flowing hair. Repeat after me.'

Assad immediately repeated it.

The next day, the schoolmaster quoted:

Who then would ever tire of seeing his breath leave his own breast?

'That was by Al Maari who went blind at the age of four.'

On another occasion he said: 'Now Assad, listen. Listen to our great poetess Al Khansa. Her two brothers have been killed in the struggle against a rival tribe; she is mourning their death:

[. . .]
The raging century
has foiled us with her treachery.
Our body it has now run through
with blows from its one steely horn.
[. . .]
Yet from today we must remain
with other men on equal terms
like rows of teeth all ranked inside
the mouths of men in adulthood.

'Did you understand all that? You would think those words were written today, wouldn't you?'

'It's time we sent that old animal off to end his days in the country,' prompted Asma, not daring to say the word 'abattoir'.

The sight of Saf-Saf, that symbol of a poverty-stricken past, increasingly irritated her.

'If Saf-Saf goes, I go with him!'

Convinced that her husband would not give in, she hurriedly changed tack.

'What I'm saying's for his own good. You do what

you like, dear.'

Any hint of scandal had to be avoided. The Christian communities were bound by their own practices; theirs – they were good Catholics – forbade divorce and barely tolerated separation. She would do better to put up with this old man's whims than to embark on a course of action which would fuel gossip and harm her family's reputation. Ever the prudent mother, Asma did not forget that she still had daughters to marry off.

A few months later, without saying where he was going, Assad spent the whole day away from home.

In the evening, when he got back, he found his donkey lying under the tree. Dead.

Had Stavros, the Greek cook, anticipating his mistress's wishes – which he shared in part – secretly poisoned him?

Assad buried his animal at the foot of the banyan tree.

He dug the grave himself. Then he placed Saf-Saf's body beside the tough, pale roots with their time-defying sap.

Following the death of his donkey, Assad would disappear during the day and return only at night.

He was doing the rounds of the souks again.

Thirty years had gone by. Many of his companions had gone. A few were left. They recognised him and greeted him warmly; not one of them said a word against him for all those years of silence.

The old man got to know Nina, the daughter of a Maltese woman he had secretly loved at one time. The girl told him what her late mother used to say: 'From the way she talked about you it was clear she was fond of you. She used to laugh when she described your donkey to me. What was he called? See if I can remember . . . Saf-Saf, was that it?'

'Yes, that was it: Saf-Saf!'

They became closer.

Assad visited several times a week. They could talk to each other; they began to love each other, despite their age difference. Whenever he went to Nina's he felt wanted, loved.

After a few months, she was expecting a child. Assad adopted him and saw to whatever the mother and son needed.

Late one afternoon, in the hansom cab taking him from one place to another, Assad breathed his last.

At the villa they hurriedly took down the yellowing photograph showing the old man, face beaming, fez askew, astride his donkey.

In Nina's home the same photograph remained, in pride of place, on the little gilded side-table.

To eradicate any reminders of Saf-Saf and any memories connected with him, Asma and her children had the cell-like room and the long corridor torn down.

They also tore down the banyan tree.

The huge, muddy scar was covered over with a large flowerbed of dahlias and irises.

More than a century later – having married into some minor families of the European aristocracy – a few of Assad's descendants, picking up on the latest fad, attempted to draw up the family tree.

They very soon stumbled against the trunk. Finding it was lowly and impoverished, they promptly put it in fancy dress.

The 'cork seller' was transformed into the son of a governor who had been elevated to his exalted position by the Ottoman Empire. As for the donkey, they turned him into a horse! Saf-Saf was given the name '*Seif el Nour*', which means 'Sword of Light'.

Thus adorned with wealth and power could the ancestor, mounted on his charger, disembark with dignity in the port of Alexandria. And, from there, set off on the conquest of new lands, for him and for his descendants.

The Weight of Things

For Janine and Willy-Paul Romain

Wheezing and muttering to himself, Olivier climbed the one hundred and twenty-one stairs that lead to his flat on the fifth floor, a suitcase dragging on each arm!

The first one contained a single change of clothes and his wash-bag. Its tremendous weight came from the pile of books, brochures, magazines and leaflets they'd been handing out free at the conference he had just been to. In addition to all this stuff, there was a fair number of manuscripts. At the last minute he had had to buy a second suitcase to fit the whole lot in.

As he struggled up the stairs, Olivier went on cursing himself: 'What on earth made me load myself up like a packhorse? To be nice? To avoid offending anyone? Because I'm weak-willed? Definitely! Because I'm stupid? No doubt about it! A lot of good it'll do you, you poor b . . ., when you've dislocated your shoulder, slipped a disk or given yourself a heart attack!'

As it rattled round the echoing emptiness of the cramped stairwell, his swearing, with a fair sprinkling of obscenities, drove him on, giving a boost to the inner man.

'I'm running on four-star petrol,' he sang out to himself as he climbed up and up, on and on.

Suddenly, as if he had stepped outside himself, he took a good look at his stooping back, his lumbering walk and his cumbersome body – all of which were well on the wrong side of fifty.

'Come on, you silly old fool, get on with it. This is all your fault!'

Then he saw the funny side of it and burst out laughing. He very rarely lost his sense of humour; like a quietly bubbling spring it would well up at the oddest moments.

Before the trip, he had promised himself that he would avoid bringing anything back. All the handouts, catalogues and brochures he would throw into his hotel room waste-paper basket; as for the books and manuscripts, he would ask the authors to send them to him by post. Although it was nothing special, the literary column he wrote in a local magazine meant that he was subjected to a constant stream of correspondence.

His good intentions dwindled away when faced with a real, live person.

He saw the ambush coming a mile off. The author would move in on him: sometimes it was with shy hesitation; sometimes with bold self-confidence. At the sight of the innocent face, Olivier was as incapable of rebuffing the hand holding out a book or a sheaf of papers as if that hand had been a part of his very own flesh.

The slightest reluctance on his part would have been tantamount to being rude and he could never do that to anyone! And anyway, he was genuinely interested in his fellow human beings and the written word. Having personally suffered from the hopes and anxieties which are the weft and warp of every page, he was very conscious of them. He knew he could never have borne rejection.

'Thank you, thank you,' he would say time after time, forgetting his good intentions, as one book piled upon another, adding to the stack to take home.

It was pity, but he had only one pair of eyes when he could have done with ten, twenty, a hundred! His time was becoming more and more limited but each manuscript deserved care and attention.

Outside his front door, Olivier dropped his two suitcases to the floor and gasped for breath before turning his key in the lock.

The small block was six storeys tall with just one flat on each floor; the dark blue gloss paint on the doors threw into stark relief the whiteness of the walls. His flat had a living room and a bedroom – and whenever he got back, he felt its gentle, sheltering protection surround him.

Night had fallen. It was one of those short days when

the town slips into darkness by four o'clock in the afternoon. The way he reacted to the disappearance of the sun depended on his mood – sometimes it made him sad, sometimes contented. He had built up a stock of remedies for life's little difficulties, so he could immediately counteract each one with something he enjoyed.

To deal with the dark, for example, he had screwed a powerful bulb into the light-fitting just above his front door and this shed a dazzling glare onto the narrow landing. That evening, feeling himself engulfed in a cloud of gloom, he lost no time in flicking on the light switch. Everything shone bright!

He started to hum to himself. He had a repertoire of golden oldies, which guided him step-by-step through his ups and downs. His neighbours, and he himself, had got used to his falsetto voice. It was just as well. He sang a lot.

In order to shake off these periods of gloom you can so easily stumble into, you have to brace yourself psychologically, like a fish as it frees itself from a grasping hand. It focuses, then flicks round with that vital energy which allows it to escape.

Olivier opened his front door. Light from the landing flooded into his hallway and scattered a shower of stars across his shoulders.

His foot stumbled against an obstacle: there they were; the books, the newspapers, the letters, dropped onto the floor by the caretaker who was always in a rush to get through her jobs.

He took a step back, heaved up the two suitcases and carried them in. Then he gazed at the mound of paper. It would chain him to his desk for hours when all he wanted to do was dream up new and original ideas – or at least he hoped they would be new and original; ideas that would be ready to take shape on large virgin sheets of paper. Ideas that any delay would drive back into the void.

He shut the door behind him. The telephone rang.

He hadn't had time to switch on his answering machine. Each ring resonated with the impatience of the caller at the other end of the line who, no doubt, had called several times. The shrill sound ripped through the air: Olivier had to stop himself picking up the receiver.

He turned on various lamps; the telephone was still ringing. It couldn't be Marika; now that she'd been promoted to senior reporter she was dashing all over the world and had told him that she wouldn't be able to phone him for at least a week

The relentless ringing was upsetting him. He rushed over and heard a tearful voice say 'Jacques' several times.

'You've got the wrong number. Wrong number,' he said.

The caller hung up; the note of distress in her voice left him feeling uneasy.

*

The heavy oak top of his worktable was covered in mail he'd not managed to answer before he left. It had been ages since he'd seen the grain of its wood and its tiny cracks stripped of clutter. Carbuncle-like heaps of books and other post of every shape and size erupted across its surface, making it look like a prehistoric animal whose slightest movement would throw everything off balance and topple its humps to the ground.

Irritation was quickly followed by curiosity. The thought of going through all this mail, catching up with friendly voices and coming across new ones, suddenly filled him with delight.

He sat down on the carpet, crossed his legs and piled all the papers up round himself. He sorted out the adverts and the invitations to events he was sure he would never get to and tore them to shreds. With his owl-head paper-knife he slit open the letters and read them avidly one by one.

Some time later he started to unwrap each book. There was a magic in the handling, reading the title and the name of the author, deciphering a dedication, dipping into a couple of pages. He spent a very pleasant hour.

Some time again after that, he opened his two suit-cases and tipped everything in them onto the floor. Paperbacks, hardbacks, leaflets, theses, manuscripts, anthologies, all tumbled out over the carpet.

He suddenly felt that he was struggling against the constantly swelling flow of a mounting sea, against a tidal-wave of ink. Blinded, suffocated by the miasma of print, he had to find a way out, an opening in this ceiling that he was about to be crushed against . . .

It had gone midnight. The pile of papers had barely shrunk. He was never going to get to the end of it! The last few hours had slipped past like life itself. He was getting on for sixty and hadn't noticed; except when that little extra exertion gave him a twinge or when he saw himself in a photo. He had always avoided mirrors; the abrupt and fleeting images they reflected were a trap, a prison.

Olivier had another quick look at the letters, books and manuscripts. How could he grant them all their wish? Give them what they wanted? How could he acknowledge them all? Even just sending out acknowl-edgements would take him hours! Hours which would gnaw away at the time he needed for his own interests, limit the breathing space he needed for friends, day-dreams, ruminating.

Suddenly he sat up straight and resolutely pushed away the pile of papers; he got up and went into the kitchen. He pulled a bin-bag out of a cupboard and shook it open. Taking it back into the living room he collected up everything lying on the floor and tipped armfuls into the yawning black hole.

The bag was soon full to overflowing. He fastened it with the plastic tie that came with it. During this final manoeuvre he suddenly had the appalling sensation of murdering a sensitive, living voice, of condemning it to silence.

As he dragged the full bag onto the landing and then bumped it down the stairs, a feeling of freedom and relief welled up inside him.

Olivier went to bed fully dressed and fell asleep immediately.

At about five in the morning he woke up, filled with remorse. He could hear a low moan rising from the depths. Turning on his portable radio he tuned in to some noisy music that would drown out the wailing coming up from far below.

He tossed and turned between his sheets. Sleep was impossible. He got up, drank a glass of water, got undressed, put on his pyjamas and tried, unsuccessfully, to sink back into oblivion.

Suddenly his body made a move. He saw this body of his leap out of bed, clamber over all the clutter, dash towards the door and dive down stairs.

He had no choice but to follow it!

Threads of dawn light were seeping through the dormer window, bathing the stairwell in gold. He hurtled down the stairs to the ground floor.

Neither the caretaker nor the dustmen had done their rounds yet. In the yard he was relieved to find his bin-bag still there.

Grabbing it round the top with both hands he heaved it onto his back as if it were a body he had come within an inch of murdering most foully!

One by one, he made his way back up the one hundred and twenty-one steps, panting and wheezing. Yet reassured, happy!

He had never been so happy!

Brothers in the Long Ordeal

For Vénus Khoury-Ghata

I

There were five of us that morning. Five young soldiers aged between eighteen and twenty-three, in helmet, boots and khaki uniform. Each with a machine gun slung across his chest. Day in, day out we patrolled the narrow lanes, our eyes constantly watching, prying. Occasionally we would nudge open a door with the tip of our gun barrel in an attempt to catch someone plotting an attack.

Yet again tension was running high in the town. Two days before, a bomb had claimed one life and injured six people; a patrol had found and then arrested the bomber.

'Those bastards, I'll make them pay,' yelled the sergeant.

Heading for the inner suburbs he strode along at the head of our group. From time to time he turned round: 'Get a move on! We've got to scare them, and now! That'll stop them doing it again.'

'We've already got the one who did it,' I said.

'And he admitted everything when he was questioned.

We know where his house is; that's where we're going!' snapped the sergeant.

'To do what? After all, the man's behind bars.'

Without slackening his pace, he stared at me over his shoulder and shook his head; he couldn't care less about anything I might say! Being a short man, he threw out his chest every time he moved. His cartridge belt, pulled in too tight, made his overweight backside bulge out at the base of his narrow back. His cap, rammed down on his head, hid his forehead and his eyes. He never unbuttoned his collar or rolled up his sleeves, so we could see neither his neck nor his arms, not even when he was at rest. It was as if the flesh-and-blood part of his appearance, the only part which did not bear the stamp of the soldier, bothered him and as if he was trying – by identifying entirely with his duties – to turn himself into a mere uniform, a mere kit!

'You there, David, stop asking questions. Just obey orders, like the others,' he shouted at me.

The sergeant pounded on, kicking up clouds of dust which smothered us as we followed him. His voice became deafening: 'Where does it get you, hesitating and arguing? Nowhere! Believe me, David, one day you'll be the one they're interrogating.'

So indignant was he that he ran out of breath: he stopped dead for a few seconds and turned to face me: 'Well, which side are you on? Can you tell me?'

'Sometimes this side, sometimes that side . . . on the side of justice,' I muttered.

Without waiting for my reply he had set off again. My comrades found this skirmish most amusing. There was no hostility in them. And no understanding of what I was getting at.

I was expecting the worst from this sortie of ours; blanket punishment for the whole district; or reprisals against the terrorist's family; or even a clumsy move, an uncalled-for word which would spark off the violence yet again. Where was it all going to end?

For the sake of my conscience I attempted to justify these punitive measures. 'We're acting like this out of panic,' I told myself. What we fear today merely adds to the fears we have inherited. 'It makes my blood run cold too, when I remember the atrocities which our race has suffered over the centuries.' I was young, I was utterly confused. I wanted to live.

The people on the other side, didn't they have good reason to be scared, too? Didn't they have the right to live in dignity? Didn't they have reasons for arming themselves against us? Aren't they merely yesterday's victims turned into today's formidable enemy? My mind was exhausted with thinking round and round in circles like this.

After marching for half an hour we arrived at the edge of the built-up area. A dozen armed soldiers were on lookout; they had been there since the previous day to prevent or to calm down the slightest whiff of insurrection. As he got nearer, the sergeant exchanged a few words with them. The stone throwing, which I regarded as a pathetic cry for help, had started up again in one area of the Protectorate.

On the way into the suburb, the sergeant perched himself on the top of a pile of gravel, straightened his back and put his chin up. All his muscles were tensed and he said, as he looked us up and down: 'Follow me. Obey my orders to the letter. That's all you have to do.'

He aimed the peak of his cap in my direction, his eyes still invisible. Despite the sun and those sandstorms which from time to time turn our region tawny yellow, and unlike the rest of us, he never wore dark glasses. As he clenched his jaws his lips disappeared. I heard: 'David, you'll stop all this fuss or you'll have to leave!'

I stayed. Will I stay to the very end, in the hope of perhaps curbing a fit of exasperation here, a burst of anger there? I was far from imagining a situation as painful as the one which was about to take place.

'Make sure your guns can be seen. You've got to put the wind up them right from the start. Otherwise it's you lot that'll come off worst.'

We were advancing, agile, backs hunched, between the low buildings. From every nook and cranny, dozens of eyes watched us. I felt these looks landing like darts between my shoulders and in the back of my neck.

In the heart of the district, the alleyways narrowed to next to nothing. I recognised the dingy house where the balcony had finally collapsed; the ochre-painted wall, even more faded now, in front of which the fruit seller used to set up his stall; the concrete bench where, every evening, the old men would swap memories. I remembered these places, clearly.

That was all fifteen years ago; I must have been eight. My mother, a widow by then, was working hard to bring me up. In those days, whenever there was a school holiday, my mother would drop me off at Aziza's house. Aziza did the cleaning in our block of flats; she and my mother were very close.

Later, when the situation had got worse, it became impossible to get from one zone to the other. Aziza was no longer to be seen in our building. We no longer did the return run.

As we move slowly forward, the past floods into my mind. Sometimes I want to stop, to go back; at other times I want to speed up our progress. I can see myself dropping my mother's hand and running towards the shack where Amin, who is my age, is playing marbles on the doorstep, waiting for me to arrive.

Then Aziza appears and asks us in. She showers us with kind words; she stuffs us with cakes full of dates and nuts. Then she wraps up a whole pile of tasty titbits in newspaper for my mother.

Aziza makes a sort of bread which looks like huge, thin, round pancakes. She tears them into large pieces, piles on goat's cheese doused in olive oil and rolls it all up together. She then holds them out to us in her fingers and says: 'Have a bite of that!' Amin and I take a bite, one after the other. I can still hear our laughter, his laughter: 'You've got the same little teeth. You leave the same bite marks in my bread!'

In the next room, the four younger children are screeching. Savouring the pleasure she has given us, Aziza leaves them to it for a few moments. Then she rushes in to settle them down.

Yes, it is Aziza's home we are advancing on. Yes, it is the same one; more dilapidated and, as I am now an adult, looking more cramped. Chunks of plaster have fallen off, leaving flaking patches on the wall. Scorched by the sun, the black fabric, which had been used as blinds on the two skylights, has turned rusty. The door, which has been repainted year after year, is still the same saffron yellow.

One of my comrades whispers to me: 'This is the terrorist's place. The sergeant's going to make them pay for that killing the day before yesterday. His father and his mother died in the camps. He's lost three other members of his family in these wars. You've got to understand him, he'll never get over it!'

II

They found Selim last night, after the bomb went off.

Bad news gets round like lightning. My young brother had gone to ground at a friend's house, very near the arcade where he had planted his bomb. We haven't seen him for months. He often changes his hideout.

After our father's death – he passed away three years ago – Selim used to turn up briefly from time to time to see his brothers and sisters and to give our mother Aziza a kiss. He is still deeply attached to her.

His face gives every appearance of being calm; but a tremor often ripples under his skin scarred by childhood smallpox. His curly, cropped hair makes him look as if he is wearing a black helmet; when he scowls, his ebony eyes flash. Sometimes he bites his lips to hold back his uncontrollable anger. My young brother dresses carefully: his jeans are old but clean, his green T-shirt freshly washed; he wears trainers; it's useful when he has to run for his life.

Selim raged against the way our father was so meek. He accuses me of preferring to talk rather than act at any cost.

Our mother begs him to calm down. He will have none of it.

'You're living like vermin! I can't stand it. I won't stand it another minute!'

*

The day before yesterday the bomb went off; one person died and three were seriously injured. Selim confessed. Our mother is in agony; she is angry at the whole world. I'm in agony too, torn between the brother I love but do not approve of and that innocent dead victim. These senseless, brutal hostilities infuriate me. I find it hard to accept that people rushing toward their own death cannot stop butchering one another.

'You're suffering in silence, but other people are doing something!' snaps my brother. 'We've been chased off our lands, humiliated for decades, reduced to having to wait endlessly . . . What have we got left to hope for? Your noble thoughts are all very well, but where do they get us? Where?'

We quarrel, we come to blows. His body tenses, his finer feelings wither. So do mine.

Suddenly he is off, glancing at us one last time with exasperation and affection. For days and days on end we hear no news of him . . .

Last night my mother and the younger ones tried to get some sleep. There are about ten of them; there are her own sons and daughters as well as the children of her three eldest. Generation overlaps generation.

I'm on watch outside. Dawn is well on its way; I can relax a bit; in broad daylight there is less risk of a raid. Before going back into the house to get some sleep myself, I spot, through a pall of dust, five armed men moving toward me.

The last part of the way they do on the double. I have no time to react. They push me out of the way to get in. I hear: '. . . the house of Selim the terrorist . . . Yes, it's this one with the yellow door. You can't mistake it.'

I bar their way: 'My brother doesn't live here any more. Don't go in! You'll frighten my elderly mother and the children.'

'The weapons . . . the hiding place . . . search the whole place!'

One of the men comes up to me in a fury: 'There's one person dead and several injured . . . one dead, the day before yesterday! Do you understand?'

I am standing in front of the door. Overpowering my attempts to resist, four of them force their way inside. I try to follow them, a fifth soldier holds me back: 'Don't put up a fight, there's no point. Just wait. They'll soon go, I promise.'

His voice is warm, almost friendly. I shake myself free from his grasp. I trust no one. I am still trying to get in, to help my mother.

The man does not let go of me: 'Don't you recognise me, Amin?'

Recognise him? I have no desire to recognise anyone in that rabble! I push the man roughly against the wall and go into the house.

I can feel that he is still behind me, hard on my heels. I rush into the bedroom. Amidst ripped mattresses, straw strewn on the ground, piles of blankets, drawers wrenched out of the one whitewood wardrobe and scattered clothes, my family is huddled together shouting and moaning. The indescribable noise adds to the hammering on the tiles round the sink where they are trying to unearth a hiding place.

'It's me. David.'

How did I manage to catch that name in the middle of all this uproar?

'No weapons, there are no weapons here!' my mother is sobbing.

'David . . .' The name strikes me like a slap in the face! I turn round and land a punch on his nose.

From a distance my mother, Aziza, is following our every move; she suddenly breaks away and bounds over to us, forcing me to step back. She grasps the soldier by the arm: 'You! You! David! I recognise you. You have always been welcome in my house, you can't let this happen. You can't. You can't, can you, David?'

David puts his arm round my mother; he lowers his eyes, he is lost for words.

Hearing the commotion, the sergeant rushes up to us: 'Get out of here, David! Stand guard outside.'

'I know this family. They were my family . . .'

'You are making things difficult. Get out of here . . . That's an order! I'm not telling you again: get out.'

My mother grasps my hand: 'Amin, you can see he can't do anything. This is all beyond him, beyond us all. Don't keep him here. Tell him to go away.'

I push David firmly towards the door. 'Go.'

'Yes, go, David,' my mother repeats. 'Go, my boy, go . . .'

'Sooner or later you'll pay for this, David!' the sergeant bellows.

III

I pace up and down outside like a caged animal.

The patrol leader has slammed the yellow door behind me.

The noises from inside which reach me are faint and muffled. I want to force my way back in and make them stop harassing these people. At this precise moment, I feel remote from my blood brothers on my side and so close to these distant brothers from the other side.

Outside Aziza's shack I am trying to calm myself. I am trying to convince myself that when the soldiers don't discover anything, they will go away again, letting the family escape with nothing more than a fright. What will become of us all? I can't see that there are any answers to my questions.

Will I see Aziza again? Will I speak to Amin? Will they understand? Will they be able to work out what is at stake in these acts of war which make us, in turn, executioner or victim, hunter or prey? Will we ever be able to remove all trace of these infernal times, will we ever make up for these shattered times? Will it ever be possible for me to run to Aziza without thinking twice? For her to accept me? Will I ever be able to share cheese-filled bread with Amin and call him 'my brother' again?

The commotion is dying down. The yellow door has just opened.

The patrol leader appears on the doorstep. In an affable voice he announces that the search is over. Then he asks the whole family to stand together, over there, at the far end of the alleyway.

Amin leads his family out; they follow one after the other. Aziza brings up the rear. I hardly dare look up and meet their eyes. But, I do so, relieved at the thought that we will soon be off. Aziza stares at me without hatred, with compassion.

As they in turn follow the frightened little group out, two soldiers brush past me and look away. The third one has not yet come out. What is he doing inside?

Then silence. An overwhelming, oppressive silence.

The sergeant's face is smooth, a lake calm after the storm. He flashes a smile at the old woman. He bends down to pick up a marble which has fallen out of one of the children's pockets. He hands the marble back and pats the child benevolently on the head. I am hopeful. I can breathe again.

At last the final soldier appears in the doorway. He joins us. He looks worried.

The house exploded, hurled into the air.

It shattered, smashed to pieces! Then, collapsing in on itself it, crumbled into piles of rubble.

The explosion was followed by a series of cracking, tearing sounds. A deadly tremor galvanised everyone in the district. They came running from all over.

Soon the shack was no more than ashes and splinters jumbled up with remnants of furniture, scraps of cloth and belongings smashed to smithereens.

Only the saffron yellow door – still standing, still intact, gaping wide open – leaned miraculously against the smoking pile of ruins.

Prison

'When earth becomes a prison cold
Where, like a bat, as hope flies off
It beats the walls with timorous wings
And strikes its head on putrid beams.'
                                        Charles Baudelaire

That was how the idea had come to her.

She had seen him lying on his back, asleep, his arms flung out, his legs apart and his chest loud with snoring.

The smoke was slowly coming out of his mouth, scrolling round his chin and round his scrubby moustache, which, she noticed, was just bits of straw, the sort used to bed down animals. Suddenly it set him alight.

The fire took a hold of the straw of his moustache, caught the straw of his eyebrows, engulfed the straw of his hair and the straw in the mattress, then everything blazed in silence.

Of the sprawling man, nothing was left but a straight, grey trail which disappeared up the hole in the ceiling, the one that served as a chimney.

She had watched the whole thing impassively.

Then it crossed her mind that she ought to get rid of

the black-haired cat, which had slipped down the front of her dress. She felt its claws on her skin. But her nervous fingers brought up only a leaf that fell to the floor with a dry rustle. A dead brown leaf. Nonchalantly, she crushed it underfoot.

She can breathe so much more easily now! The house is getting bigger. Slowly she walks to the door, opens it up flat against the outer wall. And, standing to look into the night, she begins to watch and wait.

That was how the idea had come to her. Like that, because of a dream.

This evening. She would do it this evening.

When the alleyways were filled with nothing but moonlight, lithe like a young girl, she would do it.

All that had to be done was to pull hard on the trigger. Once, twice. Her hands must not shake. Her heart, worn out by sixty years of life, and her mind, which would not concentrate, had to be focussed. There had to be an end to the hatred, to that husk to which all her memories clung. There had to be an end to that physical presence, that body, that voice and that habit of scratching his neck; that constant habit which stirred up in her some indescribable desire to crush, to destroy.

That presence; no, she could bear it no longer. It was strange and familiar at one and the same time. She would have liked the Nile to burst its banks and carry this man away, to swallow him up with the house, and with her too if needs be! But rivers, like people, would not dream of coming to your rescue.

Everything gets in a tangle, spins round and vanishes before words can take a hold. And yet at that moment, suddenly, after forty years of submission, something snapped and refused to go on. For this woman, who had never thought of packing her bags and taking off, whose long familiarity with tedious, terrifying convention had pinned her to this spot, now, suddenly, could no longer put up with any of it.

An insane hope stiffened her neck, a blade was whetted; it would slice through this fear and its demented heads.

There had to be an end to it. 'An end to it.' The phrase came back like the beating of wings. There had to be an end to it. So she could wait for what? . . . Death?

That would hardly change anything. Her life had been just that, one long wait.

She lay, unwavering, ensconced in childbirth, constant chores, the emptiness of silence and words – those empty balls that thump against the walls.

The man stretched, yawned noisily and rubbed his eyes. He had just finished his afternoon nap. He pulled himself up on to one elbow: 'I want my tea,' he said.

She answered with a nod. The water was boiling. She picked up the tin tea caddy which she kept in the corner of the room. Bending over always made her cry out in pain as she had a twisted muscle; yet she had never thought of putting the tin at hand height. The house, set apart from the village and less poverty-stricken than the rest, looked uncared for.

'Pick my clothes up and give me my slippers,' said the man.

He had sat up on his bed, legs dangling over the side, feet bare, thick toes splayed out. She put the tea caddy on the stool, went over, knelt down on the ground to look for the slippers – he would push them, time after time, under the bedstead. Her back was about to break but she stifled the cry of pain.

Still on her knees, she set about putting them on him. Then he gestured to her to get out of the way and, grunting, he shuffled over to the door.

As he did every evening, he walked though the door and sat down on the single step. There, he kicked off his slippers so that his 'feet could breathe'. Then, mouth half open, arms across his chest, he waited for time to go by.

'You put your slippers on so rarely, do give them to one of your sons,' she had so often begged him.

He shrugged without deigning to reply.

The tea was ready. She poured it into a glass. After testing it with her lips to make sure it was the way he liked it, she took it over to him.

He swilled the first sip round his mouth, swishing it from one cheek to the other, waggling his tongue, then he spat it high into the air, spattering his robe and his slippers. Their yellow leather had become stained with spots, which were now impossible to remove.

'Give them to your son,' she said in exasperation. 'You know that they're no good to you and that you're ruining them.'

He shrugged again. She had given up trying to make him listen.

'The tea's never strong enough. It's never strong enough! When will you learn to make my tea the way I like it?'

She was not listening to him. She had given up doing that as well.

There were still a few damp leaves in the bottom of the canister. She scooped them up into the palm of her hand to chew them.

When dusk fell she became restless. She went over to the unmade bed to tidy the blankets.

'Leave my bed alone!' he yelled.

As she hesitated, surprised, he said again: 'Leave my bed alone. Come and sit down!'

She walked over to the door, staring at the man's back as if seeing it for the first time. It was a wide, flabby back. There would be plenty of room to put a couple bullets into it.

When he's on the edge of his bed. When he's getting undressed, when he's pulling his long nightshirt over his head, when his head is caught in his nightshirt like a fish . . .

She squatted next to him on the step. Now their elbows were touching; in the dust of the road their feet formed a neat row.

When his head's caught in his nightshirt like a fish. I'll pull the trigger, once, twice, three times.

The rifle was under the mattress. She knew its outline by heart. She had practised bracing it against her shoulder. She would pull hard. With all her might. She tried to imagine the look on his face when everything was over. *The same face, but he will no longer be behind it.* They were sitting side by side, their black robes indistinguishable one from the other. You could barely have slipped a pin between their two shoulders.

The farm labourers returning from the fields greeted them as they passed: 'May your life be long!'

They replied with one smile; he raising his hand to his forehead, she bowing her head.

'Woman, it's getting cooler, go and fetch my cap and get my bed ready.

But suddenly he said: 'No! I'll go myself. Stay there. I'm telling you, I'll go myself.'

He had never got up to fetch anything before! He went over towards his bed, found the cap under the bolster and jammed it onto his skull.

'Why are you pulling that face? I can't do a thing without your eyes bulging like a toad's.'

Soon, she muttered, *soon you won't see my toad's eyes any more.*

A few moments later he had come back to sit next to

her. Together they watched night fall.

The last stragglers had disappeared. A hush spread
though all the alleys. The last few crows took flight and
branches played with the breeze. From the closed-up
huts rose the occasional cry from a child or an animal.

Very soon, the crescent moon would rise to the left of
the minaret. It would be time to think about going to
bed again.

The room was lit by the guttering flame of an oil lamp.
The two beds stood opposite each other: hers was a
mattress placed directly on the floor.

The man got undressed, scattering his clothes and
then kicked his slippers flying under the bed. The
woman gritted her teeth, looking at him long and hard.
He had his back to her now, his movements were getting
slower and slower. She would have all the time she
needed to take aim.

He bent down to pick up the hem of his nightshirt.
Soon the nightshirt would be over his head and it would
be time.

She turned quickly, lent over to slide her hands under
the mattress. The wood of the rifle was warm like a living
thing. She thought of it as a bird's breast with a bullet
for a heart.

Soon it would be time. Her hand was not shaking.
Her eye and her arm were young. She knew what had to
be done, she could not go wrong. She had to swing

round, take aim, count to three and fire.

An explosion ripped the air. Then another. There was the gaping wound. Its stinging pain drowned the scream. Spinning round, the target staggered and collapsed face down against the beaten earth.

The man went up and looked. He dropped his rifle next to the lifeless woman and did not notice the other weapon partially hidden under her robes.

He can breathe so much more easily now. The house is getting bigger.

Slowly he walks to the door, opens it up flat against the outer wall. And, standing to look into the night, he starts to watch and wait.

The Motor Horn

Each unto his own times past.

Suddenly, right here, in the middle of Paris, my chosen home – I am once again struck by the happiness of being able to move around in this city which excites my undying fascination and my undying love – engrossed in my walk, in enjoying myself, in being surrounded by its familiar hum and bustle – suddenly, right here, stridently slicing through the air, there's a blast from a motor horn!

And here I am, plucked up and wrapped round by the whirlwind of *that other city*.

Yet my body, my soul are etched upon this capital that I have chosen, which is where I now live. Body and soul wander near the Seine, and glimpse in passing, as if for the first time, buildings, vistas, trees, bridges – images of unfailing beauty; body and soul cross roads, go down streets, wander beneath changing skies which veer from cloudless to leaden, from watery to limpid blue; and so on and on, time after time, exhilarated by each step, delighted by each sight, and there's not a hint of nostalgia – nostalgia for that other river, for that other place, for those youthful times. Then suddenly, without warning comes a sound – a most unusual one these days – cutting across time and space; this single snorting blast of a motor horn . . . which explodes, resounds and sinks into my memory and into my bones.

Immediately everything is turned topsy-turvy and I am thrown into the centre of Cairo, my teeming, native city.

The air works its way through the capricious sands. I let myself be whisked up and then plunge willingly into a cacophony of sounds, gestures and smells. I can make out, at one and the same time, the whole fabric of the city and each of its individual threads. As I nestle beneath its outer layers, its details erupt before my eyes: the walls of the tall buildings crack and peel, the electric wires loop lazily from post to post, the uneven pavements rock beneath the perpetual throng of the passers-by. I can breathe its smell of petrol, henna, beans and spicy pancakes. Everywhere piles of workmen's stones loom up between muddy puddles.

Past and present intertwine; at a given moment, I can be any age I've ever been. I drift between the riverbanks of childhood and other alluvia, other images gleaned over forty-odd years of fleeting stays and fleeting home-comings.

I hear the hunchback street pedlar offering me sweets and shoelaces, the flow of the monkey handler's patter, the quiet words of the amputee with no arms or legs. I say hello to the lemonade seller amidst the clatter of his goblets. I recognise the newspaper vendor as he brandishes his magazines under the noses of the passers-by.

I wander and I drift. I'm at ease in this swarming Egyptian crowd which seems to swell with each step. I catch its laugh, its patient, good-natured, sensitive, mischievous glance. I recognise the rags on some, the neat, flowing tunics on others; the stiff dress of the civil servant or the baggy outfit of the student; the plump hips of a buxom woman lumbering along in her babouches; the young mother in her voluminous black robes carrying her youngest on her shoulders.

I make my way down to the main square, dodging in and out of the obstructions. The heat is dry. The noon sky, suffused by the sun, grows leaden and turns white. A human anthill hides the sides and roof of a bus which is invisible beneath the seething mass. A swarm of bicycles brushes past a line of impassive camels. Chrome-jawed cars rub shoulders with clapped-out cars and taxis; their combined impatience kicks up a storm of horn blowing.

Then – and I don't know if it is dream or reality, fantasy or routine – my first town takes a hold of me.

My life in my chosen city doesn't run in parallel to my life here, it merges with it. They're joined together. Paris–Cairo; the one galvanises the other, the one pervades the other, they are inextricably grafted together.

*

Look, here comes my father stepping out of the old, dingy brown block of flats. My father in his fifties and already a dying man.

His silver-headed cane arrives ahead of him; I can distinctly hear its every swish through the air, its every tap as it strikes the pavement.

A recent stroke has affected one half of his face, destroying its symmetry and leaving a faint contortion at the corner of his mouth. He knows he has a serious heart condition. He smiles. He's embarrassed, shy, affable; he makes every attempt to calm our anxieties, to let us be carefree and light-hearted, to avoid troubling us.

He, my father, walks on, and on, in this present-past; as if, through the mists, the car horn blew for him, but for us, too. Booming out like those lighthouse keepers' foghorns which, by their obstinate lowing, bring back each boat to port on its appointed day.

The Death of the Porter

'And yet the shadows of these lives fall on other lives,
Sweet or harsh, the one has its links to the other
As they have to the earth, as they have to the air.'
Hugo Von Hoffmansthal

Off to the left of the avenue leading down to the bridge huddles one of the poorest parts of the town. It's practically a village, criss-crossed by alleyways lined with squat, dingy houses. Behind the crudely daubed saffron-yellow door, lives Abdou, chauffeur to the banker.

That morning he was suddenly woken by a mournful wailing which sent him dashing, half asleep – with his hair tousled and still wearing his long striped nightshirt – to open his door; there he learnt that Saïd, the jobbing porter, was dead.

'The most wretched of us all!'

'He didn't even leave enough to pay for his funeral – and every nook and cranny has been thoroughly searched!'

Overcome with a fit of compassion, Zeinab – reputedly one of the best keeners in the city and normally costing a fortune to entice out to do the honours at a funeral – was mingling, gratis, her ululations with those of the neighbours.

The morning was slipping away. Abdou suddenly remembered that he had to be at work on the dot, his employer being a man of pernickety and uncertain temper. He went back inside, hurriedly dressed and reappeared a few moments later in European garb.

As soon as he had left his part of town, he was in a different world: there were avenues, shop windows, buildings that could weather the march of time. The memory of the shrill voices in his alley irritated him. But a few minutes later, as he walked along, a picture of the porter flashed before him again. He could see him in his blue cotton robe with its patches under the arms; he could see his wiry moustache and his sunken eyes. 'Saïd's got to have a proper funeral, he must. I shared my cigarette with him only yesterday!'

The banker owned five blocks of flats and lived in the most impressive, the one with caryatids adorning its façade, built at the junction where three avenues met. It was at the foot of this very building that Saïd used to squat, waiting for customers.

For over twenty years, leaning against the wall, his ropes wound round his middle, he'd been there, on the lookout for business. Occasionally he would get a job carrying some suitcases, a piece of furniture or a trunk on his back; more often he would wait to no avail. Like the chemist's window, the advertising hoarding, the florist's display or the coffee shop, Saïd was part of the décor of the block. At the very spot where he had leant for so long, you could make out a dark, indelible stain.

'For his funeral, I'll put in all I've got.' Abdou had thirty piastres in his purse. 'That's not enough,' he sighed. There were the others, of course, all the people who had known Saïd. Suppose everyone chipped in a bit . . . ? 'But I have never been able to bring myself to borrow a thing,' the chauffeur reminded himself bitterly.

It was time to decide on how best to go about asking. There was no time to lose.

'I'll start with the florist. I'll talk to him about his business. I'll say nice things about his children. Then, with a quick hint about his generosity, I'll slip in a word about Saïd.' It would be a slow job. He'd still have to talk the others into it: the Greek grocer, the hairdresser, the owner of the coffee shop, the Armenian tailor and the banker too, of course!

As he walked along the block, the chauffeur spotted the florist watering his dahlias. Spilling out of the tiny shop, overflowing their metal vases, the flowers were cluttering up part of the pavement; little Sohel, hard on his father's heels, was taking great delight in bursting the droplets of water on the petals with the tip of his fore-finger, which he then popped into his mouth.

'I'll say to him: Allah had blessed you with your sons. Their eyes blaze with intelligence. To butter him up even more, perhaps I'll tell him I'll do without the tip he gives me each time I get a customer for him: Ahmed, I'll say to him, I've thought about it and as a friend I can't accept your tips any more . . .'

Yes, that would be how to talk him round. But bodies decompose quickly! Ahmed didn't even have time to turn his head before he heard Abdou panting out: 'Saïd the porter is dead. He hasn't even left enough to pay for his funeral.'

'Goodness, well here's a hundred piastres.'

The florist casually handed him a crisp new note. Then went on watering his flowers.

'A hundred piastres! A *hundred* piastres. That's the price of six bunches of carnations . . . He's gone mad!' Pocketing the money, Abdou dashed off in case the florist changed his mind.

The Greek grocer, the hairdresser and the owner of the coffee shop all did the same. The Armenian tailor went one further: 'Take this jacket for dear old Saïd. You'll be able to cover up his own tatty old clothes.'

Things were going fast, really fast. He could hardly believe it.

'Abdou! Abdou!' stormed the banker. 'I've been watching you rushing about here, there and everywhere whilst I've been waiting by the car for a good ten minutes!'

The chauffeur dashed over and solemnly opened the car door. The banker swept in and, sinking into the far corner, yanked down the armrest to lean on.

Now came the hard bit. How should he bring up the subject with this man? . . .

'Your Excellency, Heaven has just recalled to its bosom one of your servants . . .' No, he'd have to find something better than that. 'Your Excellency, your benevolence . . .'

'What . . . ? Forty-six piastres for oil?'

His eyes riveted to the petty cash book, the banker went on: 'Why forty-six? Last week it was forty-four!'

'Everything's getting dearer.'

'You ought to be more careful. Money doesn't grow on trees, you know.'

'Yes, I know, your Excellency. But that's the going rate.'

'Going rate or not, I'm telling you to be more careful.'

How could he do it now, after that little outburst? The words which were struggling to form themselves suddenly became just a jumble in his head.

'Take yesterday, for example, I gave you five piastres. You bought me the paper and you didn't even give me the change. Where's my change?'

The chauffer rummaged through his pockets.

'It was a slip. Here it is, here it is, your Excellency.'

As he turned round, holding out the tiny nickel coins, he chanced: 'Saïd the porter has died . . . He didn't . . .'

'What? Saïd? But he was here yesterday morning. He's died? The poor man . . . ! He couldn't even have had enough to pay for his funeral! Look, here's five hundred piastres. Try and organise something for him.'

*

Everyday at lunchtime, Abdou went back home across town.

'What's got into them all?' he wondered, mentally totting up how much he had collected. 'Perhaps when they think about it, they'll get it into their minds that I was lying and that the money was for me. They're usually so suspicious . . . What does it matter! They've only got to come and see. After all, a death's a death . . . ! That much money – in less than an hour! Thanks to me, Saïd, you'll get a decent funeral.'

Abdou decided he would have a word with his neighbours before lunch. Together they would be able to decide about all the things that had to be done.

All was silent in the alleyway. To his surprise, the chauffeur met no one near Saïd's hovel. He went closer. The door was ajar. Taking his hands out of his pockets, Abdou pushed open the narrow flap of the door.

Sitting on his mattress, a plate of beans on his knees, the porter was eating his lunch.

'They thought I was a gonner!' he said and burst out laughing.

The chauffer ran as if the whole town was hard on his heels.

'Thief! Son-of-a-bitch! Police . . . !'

He could hear the banker's voice, thundering above those of all the others, pounded after him: 'I'm sacking you. You'll never get work again!'

He could see his photo and his name being dragged though the newspapers. His ears rang. 'Crook, scoundrel! He's made a mockery of death!' Saïd's laughter was goading him on but his damned flabbiness was slowing him down.

With his shirt clinging to his body and his cap clutched in his hand Abdou arrived, after what seemed an eternity, at the block of flats with the caryatids.

They were all taking their afternoon nap. The sun beat down mercilessly.

Sitting amidst his flowers, Ahmed was gently rocking back and forth on his chair, his eyes half closed, his mouth open.

'Ahmed,' whispered the chauffeur. 'The dead man . . . isn't actually dead.'

And he slipped the hundred-piastre note into the florist's jacket pocket.

'Fine, fine. Let me sleep. Tell me all about it later on.'

The florist's eyelids were heavy. Money was coming back to him, into a pocket, into a drawer. Barely a word passed between them.

Head down over a table, the Armenian tailor was snoring, his face buried in his arms. Abdou tiptoed into the shop, placed the jacket on the counter and on top of that, where it could be clearly seen, the money.

Exhausted, the chauffeur finally collapsed onto one of the coffee-shop owner's chairs.

A gentle rocking movement can dispel anxiety. Sleep sucks you down into its mossy depths.

Getting on for midnight the chauffeur set off back home. Late though it was, as he got nearer his part of town he could hear a strange uproar. He hurried on.

A little farther in he saw a crowd and had to elbow his way to get through: at the hub of the commotion was the porter's house. He struggled on, faster, choking on a welter of questions.

Outside the door to Saïd's house the people in the crowd were shouting and waving their arms about. Abdou had to push everyone out of the way so he could force his way in. Once inside the room, which was lit by a single candle, he got past first one person then another as he shouldered them aside.

At the far end of the room a thick brownish liquid was trickling from the plateful of beans and across the floor. A little over to the right, stretched out, deadly pale, lay the porter, on his back, his eyes wide open.

The chauffeur had no need to touch him to know that he was cold.

Folding his arms disapprovingly as if he'd just caught him being up to no good, he gazed at the dead man and, as if scolding him, tutted several times: 'Fool, you poor fool!' he murmured.

Then, abruptly, he fell to his knees and burst into tears.

The neighbours gathered round him. They patted him on the shoulder, for they too were overcome by the sight of so much grief. Then, to give himself time to regain his composure, the chauffeur, carefully, one by one, picked up the pieces of the shattered plate.

The Woman in Red

For Françoise and Pierre Dumayet

The bus jolted more and more frantically. Stones hit the springs of the suspension and, in a cloud of dust, flew up against the wings, struck the bumpers and rained down on the windscreen.

Angelos, the driver, took absolutely no notice. Beneath a vibrant sun he drove, five times a day, the thirty kilometres which separated the little town of Stratis from the far end of the peninsula.

On every journey, Angelos felt the same thrill of pleasure as he reached the thirty-seventh bend. From then on, he could see the sea. His Mediterranean! Dearer to him than any woman, and to which he returned every Sunday, all alone, in his little fishing boat.

During the week, life for him was one long rush. The passengers squeezing inside his vehicle became a blur in which he could not make out a single face. Crammed in, six to a seat for three, or else packed shoulder to shoulder, they clung on to the handholds, grabbed at each other and managed to cope with the jolts, the sudden stops and the awkward lurching starts.

Being regulars on the bus, half a dozen elderly women with particularly long journeys squatted on the floor in a corner that Angelos kept for them, each clutching a very young child or a basket full of food in her arms.

This crowd consisted mainly of country people and small shopkeepers going from one village to another to offer their goods for sale. No tourists knew of this route.

Most of the women were in black; the men too wore dark colours.

Amid all this dreariness, how could you miss the scarlet dress and the shining hair of the woman who had just appeared, climbing up the steps and showing her ticket before regally threading her way into the seething crowd of passengers?

The crowd parted to let her through. Making no attempt to pass unnoticed, she nodded at those around her, now and again saying the odd word which she spoke with a strong foreign accent that no one could place.

She stared self-confidently at the other travellers, smiling and thanking them over and over again when three of them got up, of one accord, to make way for her on their half of a seat.

She sat down heavily, pressing her left hand to her forehead in a gesture of extreme tiredness. But she pulled herself together at once and ostentatiously straightened up, flashing a smile to right and left at her nearest neighbours. Over her arm, despite the heat, she was carrying a huge black woollen coat with enormous, bulging pockets and on her knees she had a large overflowing raffia bag the same colour as her dress.

Her plunging neckline revealed the swell of her breasts, which were firm and full. At the end of a fine gold chain a ruby-studded cross swept, at the slightest movement, at the slightest jolt of the bus, across her milky-white cleavage.

Stunned by this apparition, Angelos stared after her for some long time as she moved past him. He stared again at each stop.

In between stops, he tried to catch a glimpse of the red figure in the rear-view mirror. The luxuriant blond mane with its dazzling highlights came down to her shoulders and partly hid her face. The gleaming shock of hair rose above the seething crowd and gathered in the sunshine.

The passengers were so crowded together that the other shapely parts of the stranger's body could not be inspected. Angelos was not the only one who felt a thrill; the whole bus was aflutter.

At each bus halt, a few passengers got off. As the woman had moved a few times, she was now sitting next to the glass partition of the driver's cab.

At one of the last stops, Angelos allowed himself a few extra moments to gaze at leisure at his passenger. He openly turned right round to look her in the face.

He could not have been more amazed . . . The dress, the neckline, the hair; until that minute they had all concealed the truth. Despite the mascara, the lipstick and the powder, this face was a good sixty years old and looked it. Wrinkles, dark rings under the eyes and puffiness had taken their toll. The shining green of the eyes was no compensation.

Angelos' gaze met that of his passenger. She had just noticed his surprise, his disappointment; it was not the first time that such a thing had happened to her. From deep within her a feeling of utter dismay welled up; she hunched her shoulders and, for a few seconds, let her head drop into her hands.

Embarrassed, disconcerted, aware that the woman was on the verge of tears, Angelos announced, in a more than usually loud voice: 'Two stops before the last one. Only two more stops!'

The raffia bag slid from the stranger's knees: her cigarettes, apples, oranges, large round loaves, chocolate, cheese . . . scattered over the floor. She hurriedly picked them all up, helped by a pale, sickly little girl.

'Have this,' she said to her, forcing the large bar of chocolate into the pocket of the little overall.

For the majority of the passengers, it was the stop before last that was the real end of their journey. It was most unusual for one of them to go any further. But Angelos always did his job conscientiously, right to the very end; he got a certain satisfaction, even pleasure, out of it. Each time he arrived, alone, at the tip of the peninsula, he treated himself to a quarter of an hour to stretch his legs.

Turning his back on the imposing fortress and its encircling watchtowers, he would wander off slowly, puffing on a cigarette, towards the sea, of which he would never tire. His thick, curly white hair covered the nape of his neck; he swayed along like a sailor, dressed like one: in winter it was a dark wool jacket, in summer a navy-blue-and-white-striped cotton jersey; and a pair of jeans did for all seasons and for all jobs.

As he was about to set off, the driver noticed that, this time, the bus had not completely emptied. One by one all the passengers had got off. All except the woman in red.

The woman had regained her composure. She was sitting up very straight and had her nose pressed to the window, gazing out into the distance.

He thought that she had forgotten where she was, that she was lost in thought.

'This is your stop,' he said directly at her.

There was no answer.

'Are you getting off?' he went on.

She turned slowly round and, staring at him, shook her head several times.

He tried again: 'This is where everyone gets off, it's the end of the line, really. There's nothing else further on.'

'I'm staying on,' she replied.

'You're not from round here, are you?' Angelos went

on. 'You probably don't realise that after this village there aren't any houses except . . .'

'I know,' she said.

'There's only the . . .'

'I know, I know,' she repeated.

Then, looking away, she sat as before, gazing out into the distance.

Nervously the driver started up his engine again; he put it in the wrong gear, felt a lurch, let the clutch out a third time. After a few jolts the bus set off again, whipping up clouds of dust around the bonnet.

Angelos had at last realised where this woman was going, despite her outfit, which he did not think was really appropriate.

It was not the first time that Giulia had taken to the road in similar circumstances.

She had come to know many a remand centre, half a dozen in various corners of the world! As soon as they released him, her son went back inside again for the same crimes: embezzlement, fraud, misappropriation of funds, breach of trust . . .

Giulia's friends had gradually lost heart. They had given up trying to understand her determination to get Marcello out of the fixes he was constantly falling into.

'Your son's nearly forty, let him sort himself out now.'

'I gave birth to him,' she would reply. 'I'll never abandon him!'

The father had disappeared without trace. Family and friends had dropped them. Giulia's meagre fortune had practically melted away.

For more than twenty years she had lived, come disappointment or success, according to the ups and downs of her son's life.

Within a few weeks of getting out of prison he would be living the high life: grand hotels, a powerful car, clothes from the best tailors, bespoke shoes from the bootmaker to the stars. But he would never fail to ask her forgiveness, to make promises for the future, to shower his mother with kindness and gifts.

He gave her, amongst other things, a scarlet dress, designed by a famous name, which he insisted that she wore on the few occasions when he invited her out: 'You'll always look young and beautiful in that, just as I want you to.'

She felt pampered, loved by her only child. In her heart she continued to feel she had everything she wanted during his long months of silence, but often she felt the sadness, the anxiety of this silence, without ever criticising him for it.

Then came the dark times. Suddenly, like a storm in a summer sky; the long-distance telephone call, the pleas for help.

Whether it was boom or bust, Marcello never explained anything; his activities remained a mystery. Giulia did not want to appear overbearing, indiscrete. She merely set the wheels in motion – the right people, money, lawyers – to help him.

She had visited many of these prisons! She had seen many a perimeter wall, she had gazed on many railings, many bars, she had signed many a visitors' register . . .

The first time, her heart had nearly burst when her son had appeared in the visitors' room with the handcuffs on his wrists. After that, she had always done her best to win over the guards, the warders, the instructors. She did not find that too hard. No matter where he was detained, everyone unanimously praised Marcello's qualities of kindness, good humour and camaraderie.

'He's never tried to escape. He manages to make everyone's life as bearable as possible.'

'He's good, is my Marcello,' she would reply. 'He's tremendously kind-hearted. He wants people to be happy. But then all of a sudden, his luck turns.'

They agreed. Giulia would leave, her mind at rest, in her tight red dress.

She felt it her duty to wear this dress whenever she visited him as a tribute to his generosity; she was also trying to prove to him that, despite the passing years, she could be a credit to him by keeping her body youthful and her movements supple. This spectacular garment, pulled taut like a corset, did the trick.

Giulia had worn away her life picking up the pieces then paying out compensation, living in hope then sinking in despair. She had left her family, then frightened off two or three lovers – after a few weeks or a few months together – for as soon as Marcello got into difficulty she ended her affairs, insisting on the sort of complete freedom that made life as a couple impossible.

Over the years, the scarlet dress had been the saving of her. As she put it on she would start to deceive herself; her composure returned, a sham at first, then a real composure which forced those around her to believe in her son's innocence. For what mother who was really worried, really upset, would have dared to deck herself out like that?

Little by little, as she got older, her body let her down.

The high heels, the shimmering fabric clinging to her skin, meant she had to make an effort each time she bent a joint or moved a muscle. She had nightmares. Her own young body, wound round in red fabric, floated in front of her, like a sail boat on a stormy sea. She swam towards it, she called it back, she fought against waves, all in vain. She never managed to draw level with it. But until now reality had been kinder to her. Giulia and her body of yesteryear had always been one.

Her hair alone showed no sign of the ravages of time. It was as thick, as soft, as silky as when she had been a young girl. She looked after it by brushing it vigorously three times a day.

At their most recent meeting, the previous week, the lawyer had been pessimistic. Because he had re-offended so often, complications had arisen in Marcello's case. She should reckon on him getting a two-year jail sentence.

'Two years. He's never had that before,' Giulia protested. 'It's too long! He won't last out. Something's got to be done, and very quickly, Mr Piraldi.'

For her part, she was ready to move heaven and earth. Her old connections, her charm, her affability had left their mark, which was still credit-worthy with a few people in high places.

'For the time being, don't let him know that anything is worrying you.'

'But don't you think that . . .'

'Swear to me that you won't, Mr Piraldi. Don't talk to him about it. Let's not distress him. Can I rely on you?'

She thought he seemed hesitant.

'Swear, Mr Piraldi. Swear to me that you won't say a word about your misgivings.'

The lawyer swore, reluctantly, with a nod of his head and a sigh.

Angelos is staring after the woman, hobbling and swaying on her stiletto heels, as she goes down the stony path which leads to the prison.

The scarlet silhouette stoops, trips, straightens up.

Sympathetically, the driver wonders whether it is a husband, a lover, an elderly father that she is going to visit, decked out and overloaded like that.

He shouts, as loud as he can, in her direction: 'Hey, you there, lady, lady in red!'

Giulia hears him. She turns round.

'I'll be back in three hours. I'll wait for you at the same place to take you back.'

She puts her raffia bag on the ground, waves her hand several times, and bellows in all the languages she knows: 'Thank you, *grazie, merci, muchas gracias, afkaristopoli*!'

Angelos' words have warmed her heart. Often she asks no more of life: words, a few simple words and immediately she feels peace, a sort of happiness.

With her free hand the woman wipes the sweat from her forehead and from her temples with a handkerchief. She dabs between her breasts. Then, picking up the bag, she carries on, her step lighter, almost buoyant.

As soon as she had signed the visitors' book, just outside the warders' lodge, the officer on duty let out that they had tried everywhere to get hold of her.

'Get hold of me! But why?'

It had been agreed that she would come on Thursday afternoons. The previous day, Wednesday, would be the day the lawyer visited. He would come from the capital, specially, in his grey chauffeur-driven limousine.

'The lawyer came yesterday, didn't he?'

The young man checked the list.

'Yes, yesterday. Mr Piraldi. That right?'

'Yes, that's right. Today's the day I come.'

'That's right. Today's the day you come.'

He did not add anything else but hurriedly pressed a button hidden under the counter to call the guard.

*

The man in the cap made every effort to break the news to her gently.

Marcello had hanged himself, the night before, in his cell.

She would not listen: 'I don't understand, I don't understand, it's not true, I don't know what you're talking about,' she said over and over, drowning herself in her own words, shaking her head.

'He's dead,' the man went on, lowering his voice and putting his hand on her shoulder.

The bag and the coat slipped to the ground. Dragged down by her full weight, Giulia dropped onto the iron bench.

Her lips twitched. She was trembling with cold and shrank in upon herself.

The man picked up the huge coat, pulling it right over her.

The red fabric of her dress and her flaming hair disappeared beneath the thick, dark woollen stuff under which she had collapsed.

The heavy material had become no more than a black heap.

An earth-like mound, shaken by tremors and from which rose a continuous moan, punctuated by the howls of a wounded animal.

The Dual-Carriageway

'The sky will open out above
So weary are we of this life
Amidst the ruins of our sleep.'
Paul Eluard

The pick-axes have been hacking away for months. Soon there will be nothing left of the area. In its place there will be a long wide stretch of dual-carriageway.

Unable to walk and with her anaemia getting worse day by day since the 'wreckers' arrived, Om Khalil has given up complaining. As she sits on the edge of her bed, her legs dangling down one side and her back turned toward the half-open window, she can hear the pounding getting closer. Her house is one of the last few still standing.

Sleep has deserted the old woman; she watches and waits, interminably, as if the bulldozers are going to swing into action at the slightest sign of weakness and suddenly break loose, crushing everything still standing, lashing out more and more viciously in a cacophony of crumbling walls, breaking glass and collapsing ceilings. Never have her eyes been so sharp, her hearing so acute.

Along with the beat of the old favourites the workmen are singing, she can hear them grunting as they pull or lift. She can make out the noise of a mallet as it falls, the dull thud of a sledgehammer tearing through a mud wall, a shovel scraping up rubble, a pickaxe striking a lump of metal, a wooden frame clattering to earth, its glass in smithereens.

If she were not there, on guard, what would be left of all these homes? In the twinkling of an eye the ground would be laid waste, littered with piles of debris. Then, the dual-carriageway, naked, huge and smooth like the hands of the idle rich!

Om Khalil's mind wanders; she imagines that she alone is slowing down the speed at which the area is being destroyed. She alone is fending off everything that drills, everything that gouges, everything that saws, everything that cuts, everything that shatters, everything that destroys. The tools will tire before she does. For she will never tire, no, never!

Dressed in white, suffocated beneath unhealthy layers of fat, her forehead as washed out as the unbleached headscarf which covers her hair, Om Khalil stares at her hands which lie like two wounded doves in her lap. Her puckered cheeks bear the traces of childhood chicken-pox; her broad nose and her thin, bloodless lips fade against her pale complexion and look like dead things. Every word she utters robs her of a little more breath.

Her eyes alone reveal her acute restlessness.

*

The men of the house leave at dawn and go off to the town to work. The women stay indoors, and drift from room to room, weary and idle. They shuffle their feet and ooze boredom.

They can summon up no interest in cooking the usual monotonous, meagre meals; no interest in their quarters where, lacking privacy, one household seeps into the next; they feed the new baby wrapped in its rags, they still the howls of its older brother, his face sticky with watermelon seeds and tears, as the others cling to their robes; they drift toward Om Khalil and they glide away, these women who surround her; they disappear only to reappear anew.

The old woman gazes into the depths of the shadows and waits for dusk and for Saïd to arrive. Every evening, between two games of football, he dashes in to see her. The moment she hears his tread on the stairs, Om Khalil's face lights up, the blood starts to flow more freely in her veins.

'You OK?' he asks as he comes in.

He's the first grandson after a whole string of girls. They put him in long trousers like a man and dress him more smartly than the others to make him stand out. His grandfather Yassine takes him regularly to the barber's where his hair is cropped and brilliantined. He's got the black, darting eyes of a sparrow; at seven, he can read, write and patter off his lessons.

'What a great game of football! We can get a proper game now.'

He's excited; he waves his arms about as he describes the new open space round the house. Everywhere's just one huge playground.

'It's a big as that . . . ! It's as high as that!'

Gone are the roofs cutting off heaven from earth, gone are the obstacles between ball and horizon.

'They've pulled down Slimane's house and the shops round it. When I kick the ball, it really flies!'

Om Khalil's lips go tight, her hands go cold, she stares at the child's bright red cheeks.

'If only you could get down, I'd show you!'

There are all these females in the house and Om Khalil's the only one who can understand him. The others . . . ? Well, they're just women!

In one bound Saïd is up on the bed and opening the window; the window that the old woman has resolutely been turning her back on for months.

'What are you doing, Saïd?'

'You can see ever such a long way. Look . . .'

Om Khalil shrinks back, walled in by her silence.

'Turn your head round a bit and you'll be able to see for yourself.'

Hasn't she heard? He leans over, puts his hand on her shoulder and says right in her ear: 'Turn your head round a bit, Grandma. Just a tiny bit will do.'

No, she will not turn round. She will not become a party to this devastation. Not even for Saïd: 'Come away from the window!'

'In your new house, you'll get better,' the child assures

her, thinking no doubt that she is too ill to move.

Sitting beside her he goes on: 'You're practically in the country over there. You'll be able to sit in the fields and I'll play round you. When it gets dark, we'll press a switch and all of a sudden we'll have daylight!'

Om Khalil keeps her head obstinately bowed. In her heart of hearts there will only ever be one house, this one. Like her memory, these walls bear the traces of the passing years.

'I'm going back outside now,' Saïd yells, charging toward the door.

Then, before he goes, he says: 'As you can't turn round, I'll call up to you from downstairs. I'll run around and I'll call out to you from wherever I am. You'll be able to hear me from all over the place! So while I'm playing, you won't be lonely any more. All the walls between us have gone, Om Khalil, all the walls have gone.'

The child vanishes. He clatters down the stairs and she hears him jump the last few steps. He's left the house. His voice rings round the room, falls silent, then peals out again: 'Om Khalil, can you hear me . . . ? Yoo-hoo! And from here, can you hear me from here?'

The old woman grimaces, raises her arm and quickly forces down the sash behind her. The window slams shut.

*

Emptiness gnawed away at everything, tightening its grip round the house. Evening after evening, pulled by little grey donkeys, cartloads of debris were hauled away.

Old Yassine surveyed the scene and shook his head. Could anyone convince him that life over there will be easier? On the new estate, the houses will be built of stone, there will be running water and electricity. Instead of neighbours helping one another, each house will be a healthy distance from the next so the air can circulate freely. Advantages, maybe, but he wasn't entirely happy about them. Water, stone, electricity, it all cost; as for the air, God only knew what price they would ask for that!

Here, everything was familiar: the warren of streets, the higgledy-piggledy houses indistinguishable one from the other, the sour smells, the puddles that never drained away, the coffee seller's wooden hut, the yam vendor's tumbledown shop . . . The move away was going to open up a gateway onto the unknown, onto danger. Who knew what? And how were they going to pay back the loan? The compensation the local authorities had paid them for this wasteland would cover only a tiny part of what they were going to buy. Then there would be other expenses!

To take his mind off these futile misgivings Yassine often felt the urge to pile everything onto a cart: his furniture, his old clothes, the twenty-one members of his family, and just leave, suddenly, like diving into the ocean.

But his wife would never agree to go with them. Could she ever agree?

'How do you feel today?' he asked, walking into Om Khalil's room.

She gave him a weak smile. He did not look well himself, despite being a big man. He had given up shaving some while ago and his moustache was growing straggly; there was a button missing on his jacket and his garish tie made his shirt look all the more grubby. His appearance would have put a taxi driver to shame.

'Look, I've brought you some medicine that'll get you better.'

'You know quite well what will get me better . . .'

He turned a deaf ear.

'Tell me we're staying here and, I promise you, I'll get better.'

He pulled up a chair and sat down in front of her: 'I've got to talk to you.'

'Talk then.'

'Are you going to listen?'

'I'm listening.'

Moving the chair, he drew a little nearer: 'It'll be our turn soon.'

'Our turn to what?'

'Our turn to leave. There's the blacksmith's house and then it'll be us. I've managed to get them to leave it to last, that's the best I could do.'

'It'll never be us.'

'You know there's nothing we can do about it, Om Khalil.'

'I'm not leaving.'

'They're going to pull everything down. We'll be forced to leave. You don't want us to sleep in the rubble, do you?'

'As long as I stay here, they won't dare touch a thing. They wouldn't dare.'

'But there's nothing else they can do.'

'I'm not leaving . . . They won't kill me for the sake of a few stones!'

Her face went ashen, her lips turned blue; she put her hand to her heart.

'Enough said,' he muttered anxiously. 'Enough said . . .'

Two days later, Yassine decided to take a different tack with his wife: he simply described the advantages of the new house, without mentioning the move.

'You know what they're saying,' he started, casually wandering round the room, 'they're saying that the new houses will last for hundreds of years . . .'

Having always refused to go and look at them, he tried hard to remember what his sons had told him about them.

'Ours has got three rooms with stairs leading up to a roof terrace. Later on, if you want, we can build some more rooms up there.'

Her eyes followed him. Taking heart, he went on: 'On the terrace you could have some chickens or a goat, I'll buy them whenever you want . . . The air's better than here. Your breathing will improve and when you breathe better, you'll get better!'

He was pleased with the way he had spoken so persuasively and as she didn't interrupt him he went on: 'We'll have far more things than here, but everything will still be the same because we'll be taking everything with us. There's the loan of course . . . ! But what's a loan when there are five able-bodied men in the house . . . ? Nothing. A speck of dust. The shadow of a speck of dust!'

Intoxicated by his own words, he ended up convincing himself, and as a finale, drowned the past in a flood of abuse.

'The dregs, that's what we've been! Is this what you call a home . . . ?'

He raised his voice, sweeping the air with his outstretched arm: 'A pigsty, more like . . . ! Like animals, that's how we've been living, like animals!'

Arms folded, head held high, eyes deliberately closed, Om Khalil made it quite plain that he was talking to himself.

At the end of the week the foreman from the building site came over and said that he had done all he could and that in two days' time Yassine and his family would have to be on their way.

'What are we going to do?' said Yassine. 'We can't use brute force to get her out.'

'It'll have to be done,' retorted one of the sons-in-law.

'Well, I'm not taking the responsibility for doing it,' said Yassine.

'Neither am I,' objected Khalil, the eldest son.

'What, then?' said another. 'You heard the foreman.'

'It would have been better had she died before it came to this,' said Khalil.

Little Saïd, who had been listening, crept up and slid his hand into his father's.

'It would have been better had she died,' repeated Yassine.

'Once she's there, she'll get used to it,' insisted the son-in-law.

'She'll never get used to it,' said Yassine. 'I know her . . .'

'She'll get worse bit by bit, day by day,' sighed the youngest son.

'She deserved an easier death,' mused Khalil.

Then, having put off their decision until the following day, they went their separate ways.

Saïd spent the last day sitting on the doorstep, hugging his football to his chest. The men were away. The women were tense; their shrill voices indistinguishable from the squealing of the younger children.

The child was sad. His heart felt heavier than the football. He regretted having spoken up for the 'wreckers', of having dreamed of the wide dual-carriageway and of having preferred, right from the start, the new house to this one.

The football fell, rolled along the ground, struck a pile of scrap metal and stopped . . . Stay where they were? No, that's not what he wanted. He stood up, empty-handed and, turning round, gazed at the stairwell. Then, having made up his mind, he went up the stairs, step by step.

The golden light of the setting sun flooded over the old woman as she huddled on her bed, supported on cushions. Her back was turned to the window. The child walked into the middle of the room, then stopped. He wavered from one foot to the other.

'Haven't you got anything to say to me?' she asked, beckoning him over.

'I don't know.'

'Tell me a story.'

'What?'

'Anything.'

'I don't know anything.'

'Say a poem for me . . . The one about the frog that stole the bride's hair.'

'I've forgotten it.'

'The one about the goose who thinks she's a swallow.'

He quickly reeled off what he could remember of it.

'That's funny!' she said clapping. 'Each time you tell

it, it's just as funny.'

Saïd didn't agree. The story wasn't funny at all. Nothing was funny. He wasn't in a mood to play any more or laugh. Perhaps he would never laugh again. Om Khalil was still clapping. The child could imagine her being forcibly moved out in a cart, he could see her haggard face, the tears running down her cheeks, her old hand clutched across the front of her robes. He would never be able to bear to see such a sight!

'You mustn't be unhappy. I don't want you to be.'

He drew closer.

'We're leaving tomorrow, Om Khalil.'

She shuddered.

Then, muffling his voice, the child said: 'So for you, it would be better if you died.'

She bent her face toward the child's and felt his sweet breath against her cheek.

'You'd be happier, wouldn't you, if you died here, in this house?'

The old woman closed her eyes: 'Yes, I would be happier.'

As she said it, she could picture Saïd sprinting across a smooth, wide road, a road just like the wide dual-carriageway. He loved her, but how he longed to get away . . . 'This house is mine; it's part of me. The other house will be the child's, it'll be part of him.' The mists cleared. Suddenly it seemed to her that she could see life from on high and as a whole, as the swallow can. 'We can love each other without being in the same house or even being the same age.' She felt extraordinarily tired. Go on struggling. For what? Against what? Against machinery, yes. Men, perhaps. But a child . . . 'Tomorrow is not for me. Yesterday is not for him.' Yesterday reeked of sickness, of her own smell to which she had become accustomed. But the child . . . 'He has to be able to breathe.'

It was straightforward, almost easy. Inside her something snapped: she felt as if she was taking a step back, that she was removing an obstacle.

One single step and, all at once, night fell.

At first Saïd thought she had fallen asleep. When he realised he could no longer hear her breathing, he knelt down and peered up into her face. She was smiling. Tracing her lips with his finger, he touched the smile. The mouth was cold.

The child knew that the smile was there for ever. The thought filled him with delight. He stood up and ran out of the room to spread the good news.

On the bottom step, Saïd met his grandfather who had just reached the house.

'We're going tomorrow! . . . Om Khalil is happy. Now she will be happy for ever and ever.'

The old woman's smile clung to the tip of his finger.

Yassine pushed the child aside.

Roughly shaking off the women who were trying to hold him, he rushed up the stairs.

He flew, taking the steps two by two, his shoulders shaken by sobs . . .

Outside Saïd fetched his football and threw it up, up into the wide-open space around him.

The Swing

For Lucienne Gilly

As soon as I can escape the eagle eye of my governess, no matter what the time of day, I rush to my swing. It's at the bottom of our garden, behind our villa which is tucked away in a residential district of Cairo. It stands just a few feet from the garden wall separating us from the surrounding streets and looks out toward the heart of the city, its back turned on our sizeable house.

The house is huge, faded. Its porch opens out onto a terrace ending in a dozen white marble steps leading down to the lawn. Three balconies, embellished with bottle balusters, are permanently deserted, eerie in front of their half-closed shutters.

Mine is not one of those swings which dangle – between two sturdy branches – from strong ropes and are free to fly up, up to the treetops. Quite the opposite. With its seat firmly gripped by two strong wooden uprights hanging from a metal crossbar it looks manage-able, domesticated. Factory built, it's like a miniature bedroom minus the walls. Obediently ensconced in its tiny space, held together in its solidly built frame, it appears wholly incompatible with flights of fancy.

And yet I rush madly off toward it, as if in for a treat. I even have a soft spot for the planks of its varnished seat, sadly peeling in places and faded from the relentless onslaught of the sun. That's where I feel at home, far from the house where I have the vague feeling that trouble, an amalgam of anger and innuendo, is brewing amongst the adults; trouble in which I want absolutely no part. At the same time, I can dodge the surveillance of the governess whose one aim in life, so it seems to me, is to saddle me with laborious musical theory or dreary arithmetic.

Once on the seat, I set off to-and-fro. Little by little the swinging movement lifts me up off the ground, giving me the notion that one day I'll get so high my flying easy chair will give me a glimpse of the neighbouring streets; perhaps even, in the distance, of the teeming and mysterious city.

This swaying rhythm is a pleasure in itself. I delight in this swinging motion, in this pitching back and forth; I savour the air which – fanned by me and me alone – plucks at my hair and whips against my face. What's more, I enjoy the isolation; it's a vibrant, productive isolation and I'm learning to use it to my advantage.

It's from within this silence, from within this detachment that I gradually become aware of the incongruity of fate and of my own existence.

'Me . . . Me? . . . It's me that's *here*,' I say to myself. 'Who is this me ? What am I doing on earth? At this point in time, in this particular country? And why?'

I have the enthralling feeling that, thanks to an infinite number of happy coincidences, I own a fragment of life. I know how precarious it is; I have learnt that death is all around and never far away. I am both infatuated and petrified by the privilege of being alive: 'I might well have never existed.'

As I ponder, my arms, my top half set to work by themselves. They hold me aloft in joyous swoops back and forth.

I know how fragile I am, so fragile . . . And yet so strong.

Far behind me, the house is teeming with activity. Tomorrow they're putting on a big reception.

My questions go unanswered: or at least, the answers are hard to pin down, just as what's happening on the other side of the garden wall is all a blur.

I'm not too worried. I'm convinced, even at my age, that all that's needed is to nurture, to feed the questioning and the yearning in your heart of hearts for them to go on existing and evolving.

The lawn looms up and rushes away. The rings clamped round the crossbar squeak; the wood groans. But my swing will never let me down; it will go on for a years to come, giving me time to grow up.

*

It was one stormy morning – so rare for our town, huddled in the desert – that I made a pact with my eleven-year-old self as I then was.

The rain is pelting down. The flashes of lightning and gusts of wind thrill me. I'm soaked to the skin. I'm on a raging sea; I'm driving the ebb and flow of the swing. Despite the storm and the heavy swell I'm holding my course.

I am at one with my soul, with its turmoil and its bursts of energy. The adult world murmurs in the background – masks, traps and distrust are all it has to offer.

To myself I say over and over again: 'I swear to you I'll never change.'

Thus binding myself, for ever, to my childhood.

Casting itself far and wide – without ever leaving the earth – the swing will now unfurl its freedom, its fervour and its hopes as it swoops and climbs across time, across distance.

The No. 9 Tram

For Nicole Czechowski

The depot for the No. 9 tram is on the edge of town, near where we live. Every morning, at seven, I clamber leisurely aboard, knowing that I'll always get a seat as I set off for school.

A few seconds later – or a second or two earlier – a lady in her fifties gets on. In the few minutes between the depot and the third stop we have the whole tram to ourselves. We make sure we sit in seats well away from each other. She goes to the back, I to the front; or vice versa. There are just the two of us.

I'm sixteen and won't be a schoolgirl for much longer. Next year I'm off to Europe where I'll be going to university. I'm raring to be gone. In my imagination I make all sorts of discoveries, meet all kinds of people; and there's always a hint of love interest somewhere in there. It's waiting for me, in a place far from here, and one day, soon, I'll just bump into it. It will be swift and lasting. In my mind, naïvely, I associate these two words, convinced that my self-confidence will shape my whole existence. A bountiful future stretches out before me;

I'm wild and frivolous and hurl myself blissfully towards it!

During the journey I wonder about the other passenger, slumped in her seat looking grey from her hair to her clothes, even down to her skin. I weigh her up sympathetically, inquisitively. Sitting at the far end of the space which separates us, I find she's easy prey. I'm almost ashamed. As the rattling of the tram shakes us about, as the wheels screech against the rails, I can't prevent myself examining her, drawing her out of her dreary little world, conjuring up a different life for her elsewhere.

By about the fifth stop all the empty space has gone. The growing crowd has reduced it to the size of a pocket handkerchief. Soon I'm hemmed in on all sides and, as I clutch a metal pole with both hands, I lose sight of my fellow passenger. No doubt she's succumbed to being swallowed up in the swarm of people. No doubt, like me, she's given up her seat to a pregnant woman, or to an old lady shrouded in black, or to a younger one with her veil carelessly drawn across her face, or to one of the numerous cripples who are such a familiar sight in our city.

Extricating myself with difficulty from the thick, shifting magma of humanity, I get off the tram practically at the end of its run. As yet I don't know where my travelling companion gets off. (I call her Denise, I really couldn't say why.) Perhaps she's just ahead of me. This mass of men, women and children obscuring the sides and the windows of the tram screen everything outside from view.

The following day we're back in our usual places and I pick up my examination from where I left off.

Around this Denise, whose voice I haven't even heard yet, I'm constructing a life so dull, so lacklustre, that I feel her whole existence is in danger of melting into thin air.

Her iron-grey hair, her stony features, her leaden eyes and bloodless lips repel light. An aura of infinite sadness surrounds her; a sadness which fascinates and enthrals me. She seems to have buried her real face deep within herself as if she's listening, as if she's waiting; for a plea, for an entreaty.

I've invented an unrequited love for her, a nondescript existence which, from time to time, I try to enliven with surreptitious little make-believe moments of happiness, with fleeting smiles . . . Alas, my efforts turn to ashes; I can graft not one happy picture on to her features.

Has she noticed what I'm up to? I wonder. For the past few days – as if to avoid any possibility of meeting face to face and to prevent me looking at her – she gets on the tram before me and sits in the single seat immediately behind the driver's cab. Thus she has her back to the rest of the tram.

I feel both rebuffed and relieved, for there are times when I get the impression that, were it not for this distance between us, I might be running some very real risk. I have the curious feeling that, by some strange power, this woman holds the course of my pitiful fate, and that she herself – now that she's aware of it – is trying to protect me from it.

I'm confused and ill at ease and so I pull a novel out of my satchel and bury myself in it, knowing full well that I won't be reading for long. As soon as we get to the fifth stop the crowd of passengers will force me to stuff it back in my satchel along with all the other books, pads and papers.

One morning, by chance, we happened to arrive at the door of the tram at exactly the same moment. We bumped into one another right by the bottom step.

Denise apologised with such a self-effacing, soft voice that I stepped back, embarrassed, to let her pass. She insisted that I get on first; I wouldn't. Putting her hand on my shoulder, she pushed me firmly towards the steps. Finally I gave in and muttered a few words of thanks.

This short, simple give-and-take had nevertheless spun a few gossamer threads between us. Following this exchange we both felt obliged, from then on, to shorten the distance between us once aboard the tram. Now taking seats quite near each other we would swap a smile and, later, a few words. Next, as before, we would get up to give our seats to anyone older or more weary than ourselves. Then, carried along by the crowd, we would lose sight of each another.

*

After about a week we found ourselves sitting on the same wide seat: 'Nice day,' I started.

'Very nice,' she replied.

'It'll be very hot later,' I added. In this city with its fiery sun, the comment was remarkably trite.

She replied just as conventionally: 'Yes, very hot.'

Encouraged by this fugue for two voices, I ventured: 'Do you always get on at the depot?'

'I live right near it, which is lucky.'

'So do I . . . I get off at the school. What about you?'

A tremor ran through her lips. She lowered her eyes in an attempt to control the storm of emotions which buffeted her whole body. After a long pause she opened her eyes again, looked straight at me, summed me up – then said in one breath: 'Every day, I go and see my son. He's a dancer. A great, a very great dancer.'

Wave after wave of passengers filled the tram. I could see her hanging on to a pole, to a seat-back as, yet again, she was jostled away, pushed back and forth by the crowd. Her pleading eyes seemed to be looking for me. It was as if she were drowning, as if I were her one remaining lifebuoy.

I shouted a few words to her over the head of the scrum: 'Tomorrow, I've got a day off . . . Tomorrow, can I invite you out. We can go to the Café des Pigeons. Meet at three.'

Both on the way into town and coming back, our tram passed the Café des Pigeons down by the river. Because of its name, because it was so near the water, because of its well-spaced tables with their red check cloths, I was attracted to the place. I had promised myself I would go there one day. My savings would easily cover the cost of our drinks.

As she waved a hand above the mass of heads and shoulders she shouted back: 'Thank you. Thank you! Outside the depot, tomorrow, three o'clock.'

Some time after our congenial meeting at the Café des Pigeons, I insisted upon going with Denise (she was, in fact, called Rosie) on one of her daily visits to her son.

With its imposing covered entrance and its latticework balconies, the private clinic looked like a massive, middle-class, turn-of-the-century house, its terracotta walls and green shutters faded by the sun and the passing years. At the far end of the garden, standing on yellowing grass, amid mildewy bushes, surrounded by scrawny, ancient eucalyptus trees, there it was that I first saw Edouard.

Despite the heat he was wearing a cape cut from a heavy purple fabric. As he walked the cape fluttered around his body at each step; or if he spread his arms it would billow out like the wings of a bat. Each of his movements, each of his slow pirouettes had a grace, a rhythm, an elasticity which fascinated me. Edouard would press down his bare, leather-sandal-clad feet hard against the earth before propelling his body upward. It looked as if he were trying to stir the air, to rend it apart with a gimlet, to fashion it into a vortex, to engrave it with his soaring movement, the movement which would raise him, at last, out of his own human form.

Despite the scrunch of our shoes on the gravel, the young man kept his eyes fixed on the ground, pretending not to notice us.

Gradually he raised his head, flung back his mane of hair, tipped up his chin and slowly but surely revealed his face to me.

It was in this face that I caught sight of all the beauty, of all the distress of this world; his eyes were of an unbelievable, indescribable green from which I will never again be free.

But already the dancer was turning from us, indifferent, distant, off to take shelter elsewhere; in a place which, no doubt, appeared to him more real than anything that we could offer him from our side of things.

Rosie called out to him: 'Diochka, it's me! It's Mother.'

Then she whispered to me: 'He doesn't react to anyone, not even me. But I'm positive he can hear me, that he listens to me. Especially when I call him Diochka. . . He loathes the name Edouard.'

We went over to him; at each twirl, his cape brushed against us. Several long minutes passed and then he gazed, first at his mother and then, pointedly, at me. After what seemed to me an eternity he flashed me a few furtive smiles. Then he nodded in my direction, in an earnest invitation to join his dance.

I hesitated. I recoiled slightly. Rosie grasped me by the elbow to prevent my retreat. But suddenly, impatiently shaking off her hold, I ran toward Diochka's open arms, overcome with dizzying happiness.

Did I have, without admitting it even to myself, a heart which had become too obsessed or too riddled with daydreams? Was it, within me too, the rejection of suffocating reality – from which I had asumed I could escape by running away, by going into exile – which hurled me so suddenly into this mad dance?

I placed my hands in those of the dancer. He drew me to his breast, my cheek to his cheek.

We spun around and around, whirling amid the intoxication, the rapture of this relentless *pas de deux*. Our legs, our hair and our breath entwined. I saw, once or twice, his lips part . . . Was he about to speak?

The purple cape enfolded us. As we embraced we became but one single self.

I gave up the idea of going away; now I can go as far afield as I need.

Every afternoon I make my way to this shady, eucalyptus-scented garden. I have bought sandals just like Diochka's and a large flowing skirt cut from a heavy blue fabric. With each movement, the air stirs its folds in graceful ripples.

Rosie has left us; she has flitted off to distant cities. Knowing her son to have a regular visitor has freed her of her burden of anxiety and love; she has escaped for the very first time. She writes to us often; she sends us photos from here, there and everywhere: Paris, Mexico, Montreal . . . She is rediscovering long-lost family, making new friends; she appears more cheerful, younger.

As for me, I stay with Diochka. I'm on the look-out for those sparks which, from time to time, pierce the opaque green of his eyes; I'm watching and waiting for those imprisoned words which one day will burst through all the barriers.

'He will talk, one day, won't he, doctor? He will talk!'

The doctor shrugs; it's an odd business, the prognosis is far from clear.

On the other hand, I sometimes wonder whether it wouldn't be better to abandon Edouard to his inner music, not attempt to draw him from his silence. Deep within his inner landscape, within his perpetual dance, he is perhaps better off whirling to his own rhythm – the rhythm of the universe; perhaps he finds it easier to step into that constellation where the brevity of time and its effects are left far behind.

But there are times when my whole being cries out and rebels against such capitulation.

I no longer know, I waver . . .

The Punishment

The governess never slept well.

At three o'clock in the morning, before dawn one sweltering hot day, she switched on her bedside light and got up.

Barefoot, in her nightdress with its thin mauve stripes, she made her way across the huge bedroom we shared and came up to the bed where I was sleeping as soundly as only a child can.

Swirling round my bed, she spun a strange dance with those light, determined steps of hers and wove her presence into the shape of a snare. Her long, piercing gaze worked its way through the blue blanket I had wound round my head, puncturing my downy dreams, peeling the night from me, layer by layer, forcing me to lift my head and sit up, bleary with sleep, on top of the tumbled sheets.

'Trust you! You were asleep!'

Her attack left me unable to say a word. She persevered: 'What about your homework?'

Still speech failed me. I thought how lucky my brother was to be in his boarding school overseas, far from the battering of 'Mademoiselle's' moods.

My parents flitted from place to place, mixing with the

smart set. This barely left them any time to worry about how I lived my life. Having made sure I had a governess, they were convinced that they had done the best they could for my education. This woman was to be constantly at my side. I had always been a frail sort of a child. She was to look after me and help me with the very few but taxing lessons I went to at a private school.

Mademoiselle's erect bearing, mawkish, pale eyes, dull hair, severe clothes and lace-up shoes set their minds at rest. They were young, handsome and blasé – they left me in her hands and vanished into their own whirl of cares and pleasures.

I was eleven and wearing my heart on my sleeve – ready to love and to make myself loved by the first person that came along. But suddenly, when I saw the governess, something in me slammed shut.

Her face might have softened my heart because it was so pale, her eyes because they were so sad or her floppy curls – held in place with tortoiseshell hairclips – because they were so unruly. But there was that mouth, those lips, or to be more precise, that tight mouth, those thin lips . . . Those callous features, hewn out of flesh, chilled me.

'Get up!'

I was up. Her hair – a mass of little snakes writhing round her curlers – and her gimlet eyes frightened me. With her foot she nudged my white sandals toward me.

'Put them on before you get cold.'

I used to love the feel of the cool floor-tiles beneath my feet.

'It's summer.'

'Summer's when you catch things, you little fool.'

Mademoiselle raised her arm to hit me but held herself back by the same convulsive movement. Her struggle for self-control sent tremors coursing through her body.

Our quarters were separated from the rest of the spacious flat by a very long corridor. I sorely missed the presence of my brother – that tight bundle of muscles – in the bedroom next door and the fact that he would have yelled and kicked up a fuss at the slightest hint of a threat.

We lived right in the centre of Cairo, on the seventh – and top – floor of a comfortable but run-down block of flats. Our French windows opened onto a huge, open circular terrace which looked out over the whole neighbourhood and even had a view of a part of our dusty, magical capital city.

Having sat herself down, bolt upright, on the velvet upholstery of the wing chair Mademoiselle would grumble about the unhealthy climate. She regularly asked herself what on earth she was doing in this chaotic, epidemic-ridden country, coming as she did from a neat little town in the foothills of the Savoy mountains where she had spent her youth.

She beckoned for me to go over to her.

'I've got cramp. Massage my legs for me.'

I knelt down, torn by conflicting emotions. On the one hand I was incensed by this dictatorial attitude, but at the same time I was touched by the inner suffering and tragedy which bedevilled the governess and which I could not understand, try as I would.

I rubbed her legs with a eucalyptus-scented liniment which she handed to me. I did my best to smooth away the stiffness in her tendons and loosen the muscles in her calves.

Bit by bit, I became engrossed in what I was doing.

'Is that any better?'

She snatched her leg away: 'That'll do.'

I got up and quickly went over to my bed, longing to curl up in it again.

'And what about your chemistry homework? . . . You must tell me what you've learnt, now, this minute!'

She bombarded me with questions and showered me with formulae. I couldn't come up with a single answer.

'Hopeless, you'll always be hopeless! You're an ass, that's what you are, an ass! . . . Well, I've got a surprise in store for you.'

A look of triumph flashed across her face before she disappeared behind a chintz curtain.

A few seconds later she reappeared, ostentatiously holding a little brown attaché case which she put down on the low table in front of me.

I remembered having seen her open and close this mysterious box: I'd seen her piling in sharp implements such as blades and scissors; shoving in the odd piece of string and bits of wire.

'Open up your eyes, you'll see . . .'

I was petrified. I couldn't utter the slightest sound, the slightest cry for help. And anyway, who would have heard?

'You'll see!'

Her whole face was radiant. The blue of her eyes deepened. Her nostrils quivered, her hands fluttered and her skin went pink. It made her appear almost attractive. For the first time, she smiled at me.

At first it was a smile, then a laugh, but her lips were invisible.

Once again she became a terrifying sight.

Making passes like a magician, Mademoiselle pulled from the jumble a bright red object that she waved in front of me.

Eventually, I could see that it was a red satin hat with two enormous, stiff donkey's ears made out of the same shiny fabric.

'You see, little girl, you're a dunce. So here's what's waiting for you!'

I didn't know what she was intending to do. I pulled back at first. Then, gathering my wits about me I tried to strike a bargain with her, suggesting that, instead of doing the incomprehensible chemistry, I could recite a few of La Fontaine's fables, list the victories won by the French Empire, talk about one of the French regions or describe the whole of Egypt, our 'gift from the Nile'!

'Who is giving the orders here?'

I lowered my head. But in spite of this gesture of submissiveness, something inside me sprang to life. Something indomitable and rebellious was forcing its way into my consciousness without my realising it.

'I've made this donkey hat just for you. I've been working on it for a month or so. A couple of weeks ago I measured your head for it, do you remember? Now, it's up to you: either you learn your homework and in an hour from now you tell me what you have learnt, or you put this hat on and I'll stand you out on the balcony. All the neighbours will be able to see you. You'll be the laughing stock of the whole district.'

She gave a sudden laugh, showing her stained, decaying teeth.

'It's up to you!'

I walked toward her calmly and, in a gesture of bravado, took the hat from her hand without a moment's hesitation.

Then, standing in front of the mirror, I jammed it on my head, pulling it right down to my ears.

She stared at me, dumbfounded.

Next, I picked up the stool, tucked it under my arm and took it out onto the terrace.

Finally, putting the stool in the centre of the tiled floor I climbed onto it and stood motionless, my back straight and my head held high, defiant before the whole city.

*

It was not long until the blazing light of dawn fanned out around me.

In the building next door, an early riser caught sight of me and spread the word. Soon other neighbours and their children were peering out of their windows. The people huddling on the terraces, where the poorest families lived together, rushed up to the railings to get a look at me.

Behind me I could just hear my governess's voice. It had become suddenly shrill: 'Come back in. That's enough of that.'

I was riveted to my stool. Nothing would have prised me off.

Having swept aside all shame, overcome all fear and broken free of all shyness, I felt good. I felt free.

Life had just turned topsy-turvy. I found I had unknown strengths. When put to the test I could cope, I could rise to the occasion: I could face any monster!

The sun spilled over the tiled floor. Everywhere children were clapping enthusiastically at the spectacle I was making of myself. I could have sung with joy. In fact, I did sing, goodness knows what. At the top of my voice!

Aghast, Mademoiselle called me in, her voice getting more and more apprehensive, more and more faint.

I still wasn't giving in.

Then, suddenly, I heard someone sobbing.

It was then that I leapt down off my perch and rushed into my bedroom.

*

The governess was in tears.

Astounded by her sobs, I went over to her. Standing on tiptoe, I tried to pull her into my arms.

'No, you mustn't cry. You mustn't.'

'If only you knew . . .'

'What? What is it?'

She said again: 'If only you knew, if only you knew . . .'

Still not understanding, I finally said: 'I know. Please don't cry.'

My answer calmed her down.

The donkey hat had fallen to our feet. I picked it up and kept it cradled against my chest. She made no effort to take it from me.

As if it were a secret which, at last, we could share, she muttered: 'Keep it, to remember me by. Always.'

Not long after, Mademoiselle left us, without a word. To my great relief I was sent to boarding school.

Years later, I learned that the governess had ended her days, taking her secret with her, in a home tucked away in her peaceful native valley.

I still keep that strange headdress, buried deep in my wardrobe and in my thoughts.

I owe so much to the governess's handiwork. So much.

The Woman in the Taxi

'. . . where there is nothing shared, nothing is real.'
Martin Buber

Outside the plate-glass doors of the Grand Hotel, the tourists are queuing on the pavement.

At the wheel of her dark-liveried taxi with its white wings, Mounira draws up beside the customers at the front of the queue. A couple, she barely glimpses them, dive in; she'll have plenty of time during the trip to find out about them.

Mounira likes to create some sort of bond with the people she carries and to tease their faces out of their anonymity. Faces which she will bring back to life later on, along with other ones, according to the whims of her memory.

The movement of her vehicle, constantly brought to a halt when the stream of cars jams solid, will give her the chance to have a good look at them; to talk to them even. For Mounira, who has been in the trade for more than ten years, knows snatches of several languages, a whole arsenal of words which she rolls and jiggles around enthusiastically to create her very own resonant, all-purpose language.

*

The two people sitting on the back seat would not stand out in a crowd of holidaymakers. Swathed in cameras, armed with a guidebook and large bags for their shopping, they're off to the souks.

Like the others in the queue, they are surprised to see a woman taxi driver. Here, the practice is not very common, but recently there have been more and more of them.

Despite the protests, the jeering and the warnings of her family, Mounira, widowed at forty, had run up debts in order to embark, somewhat in the dark, on her adventure. Once she had made up her mind, she was surprised to see that, little by little, acceptance of her activities was growing and that women were openly daring to show they approved of her.

Just shaking the habit-tree is often all that is needed for the shattered boughs and the wizened branches to snap off and crumble away to dust. New shoots, then, can sprout from old trunks more easily than is thought.

Just touching her cab gave Mounira physical pleasure. Whenever her hands set the lifeless machine in motion – via the steering wheel, the steering column and the transmission shaft – she freed herself from the burden of a whole inflexible past.

She had even built up an intimate knowledge of the engine and could name all the parts. She could identify the cause of a breakdown, unscrew the air filter, make the alternator work and loosen off the disc brake, thus mastering the mystery that is car mechanics.

Putting her skills to the test, Mounira delighted in clipping the curb as she took a corner and hacking her way through the welter of traffic, the speed of her reflexes stunning her passengers as they were bounced around on the sagging springs of the back seat. She took great pleasure in skimming past other vehicles and driving elbow to elbow with other motorists, stopping dead within a few centimetres of a pair of bumpers. She prided herself on being able to wriggle her way, with a few deft manoeuvres, into a space in a row of closely parked cars.

Mounira knew every twist and turn, every nook and cranny of Cairo. To her it was a colossal ship bearing its cargo of nine million souls, of which she was one; to her it was a gigantic body packed with tiny veins through which she would expertly work her way.

When the tourist traps along the pavements bored her she would liven up the tour by having a passing word with the shopkeepers: she would say hello in turn to the bean merchant, to his cousin the knife-grinder, to the moustachioed locksmith, and a newspaper vendor on the prowl for customers . . .

The next time round she would call out to the traffic police by name. The men would answer her back, sometimes good-naturedly, sometimes grumpily, depending on their mood or their temperament. There was the misogynist on the place de la Nation who was unfailingly contemptuous; there was the kindly chap in the rue du Commerce who flashed his smiles indiscriminately; the sleepy one at the carrefour des Jardins who nodded gently and raised a cotton-clad forefinger to sort out the uninterrupted flow of traffic; there was the pervert on the avenue de la Gare who treated her to lewd remarks to which she retorted in kind.

Mounira had inherited from her mother a whole fund of ripe insults that the latter saved specially for her immediate entourage. As soon as she moved outside her intimate circle, she assumed a gentle voice and partially veiled her face.

When the itineraries she had agreed on with her passengers got too dull – and if a feeling of trust had built up between them – Mounira would buck herself up by making a dash towards the Nile, an incursion into the desert or a foray to the poorest districts.

The male passenger today has a scowl on his face and is tight-lipped; one look and you no longer existed. Mounira examines him in the driving mirror. Sitting on the edge of the seat, he avoids touching anything, avoids the risk of being contaminated by anything.

Like Mounira, he is about fifty. Short cropped grey hair. His neck twitches spasmodically. Judge-like, he notes one by one the seething images of the city.

The woman seems younger. Fairly good looking. Her face is both distant and sensitive.

Whenever her companion is engrossed in a guidebook or fiddling with his cameras, she leans out of the window and appears to be taking in the whole street. But he immediately gestures to her to wind up the window and, catching her elbow, draws her back inside, into the shelter of this metal box on wheels.

The woman lets him have his way. But a sort of gloom spreads across her face and stays there.

Then they whisper together, thus putting up a barrier between themselves and the driver.

Depressed by what she sees, Mounira unlocks the sunroof and slides it back. A whole swathe of sky opens up.

Look at my town! Look at all these people, this country . . . my great landlocked ship pitching and rolling, inundated by these voyagers.

Mounira longs to shout all this out, but who would listen to her? Leaning against each other her two passengers are now comparing postcards.

An enormous spider has woven her web over my city. Threads from her toils dangle down buildings, grasping at the streetlights and stifling the bushes; its grey fibres slither from the terraces to the ground. Look at my tattered city, my city with its din and its flies.

It is not because she wants to scare them off that she shows these things to the tourists who are obsessed by gods, myth and history. It is to win them over, really, to make them feel something.

I'm telling you about now. Listen to me! Our homes are spewing out their innards; the fronts of our houses are cracked and crumbling. We can't cope with time any more as it gnaws away, stone after stone. Beneath the feet of our heaving masses the tarmac is breaking up, wrenching itself apart to expose yawning cavities criss-crossed with rusting, leaking pipes.

These strangers, once they are out of their hotel-islands, what are they looking for, what do they see? Mounira is always tempted to stop the cab and to wade into the crowd, on foot, with them; to push them gently by the elbow into the living flesh of this disarming city.

Step into my town! Rub shoulders with the people. Mingle with these solid crowds endlessly marking time beneath a pale sun burnt out by its own radiance. Wait patiently with those who wait patiently. Set off on your journey hours before you need to set off. Force your way onto the overflowing buses, worm your way through the tangle, push your head or your arms out of the windows or else plaster the sides and the roof with your thronging bodies. Rumble on and on, in the blazing heat; or jump off when the vehicle grinds to a sudden halt because the radiator cap has flown off, catapulted into the air by a jet of muddy steam.

Words well up in Mounira's mouth; perhaps they will cut through the silence, perhaps they will find their way under the skin of this woman with her probing gaze.

Flounder through these avenues cluttered by cars, bicy-cles, horse-drawn carriages, handcarts and barrows pulled by donkeys. Plunge into this anthill over which, here and there, loom trays of pastries piled high and borne aloft by invisible hands. Steep yourself in the sheer number of people through which porters thread their way, wedged into a consignment of cardboard boxes tied around their waists. Sweat and stoop with those who carry here, those who lug there . . .

In the mirror, the contrast. The two faces in the back are no longer flesh and blood; they are mere glints of light.

Just look at how they bustle about without jostling, how ready they are to give way to you. Behind the suffering and the poverty listen to that gale of laughter, their laughter . . .

Suddenly Mounira's own laughter bursts out and startles her passengers. Embarrassed, the man gives a discreet cough.

Shortly after, the woman leans forward, puts her hand on the back of the front seat. It looks as if she is going to speak . . .

But suddenly, they come to an abrupt halt; gridlock. Once again the cab stops amidst the din of car horns.

A thin-chested lad, his head shaven, thrusts his arm inside the cab and dangles loops of jasmine right in front of the noses of the two tourists.

The woman puts out her hands towards the flowers.

The man asks: 'How much? . . . *Combien?*'

With the tips of his fingers, he drops a few small coins into the outstretched palm, avoiding the slightest contact.

Delighted, the woman buries her nose in the heap of fragrant petals. The man shows his disapproval by pulling a face. She immediately puts the white loops around her neck.

The cab moves off again. Mounira would like to look round.

Listen to me! I'll talk to you about people who are alive.

Who is alive? The woman's face is caught in the driving mirror. What ties are bothering her, what loneliness is gnawing at her? How can she be made to hear the words: *I feel close to you, stranger. Speak to me and I will speak to you.*

Thousands upon thousands of people swarm around the main square which broadens out towards the souks.

Mounira puts her foot on the brake and stops. Turning round she faces for the first time – without the driving mirror as mediator – the couple she is driving.

A speckled mauve veil covers the driver's hair and frames her smooth, strong face. For an instant her gaze plumbs the depths of the other woman's gaze and sinks into the stranger's indescribable sadness.

*

Time is getting short. The man gets out of the taxi.

Tearing a hole in the bodice of her dress in her haste, Mounira unfastens her brooch with the blue stone and pins it on to the young woman's blouse.

'*N'oubliez pas l'Egypte.*'

Leaning over the meter, the man turns his head just as his companion, deeply moved, is leaning over towards the driver to kiss her.

'*Combien?* How much?' snaps the tourist irritably.

Mounira slams the door that the woman has just stepped though and steps on the accelerator. She drives off.

Her cab is quickly swallowed up in the stream of all the others making their way to the hotels.

The Translator

Suzanne Hinton has a BA in French from the University of Wales and a PGCE in teaching French. She was awarded a Licence ès Lettres from the University of Lille and a Diploma in Translating from the Institute of Linguists. She has worked as a translator from French to English, specializing in literary texts, and regularly translates book reviews for the French Institute in London.